Praise for Susan Trott:

"Trott breaks a lot of literary rules but is able to get away with it because of her dynamic writing style."

—*Rocky Mountain News*

"As a writer, Trott isn't like anybody else. She is funny, willful, insouciant and original. She has a love for words and can make the language hum."

—*Chicago Tribune*

"Trott is a master at revealing madness in the mundane [and] lucidity in the lunacy of our lives. Her keen yet sensitive eye for human self-deception and her unpredictable wit will immediately engage and continue to surprise her readers."

—*Bloomsbury Review*

ALSO BY SUSAN TROTT:

The Holy Man

Divorcing Daddy

The Exception

Pursued by the Crooked Man

Sightings

Don't Tell Laura

Incognito

When Your Lover Leaves...

The Housewife and the Assassin

Mr. Privacy

Tainted Million

Tainted Million

by Susan Trott

RUSSIAN HILL PRESS
SAN FRANCISCO

Russian Hill Press, San Francisco
 Published 1996
Printed in the United States of America
00 99 98 97 96 5 4 3 2 1

Library of Congress Cataloging-in-Publication Data
Trott, Susan.
Tainted Million / by Susan Trott
-1st ed.
[96-069880]
CIP
ISBN 0-9653524-1-2

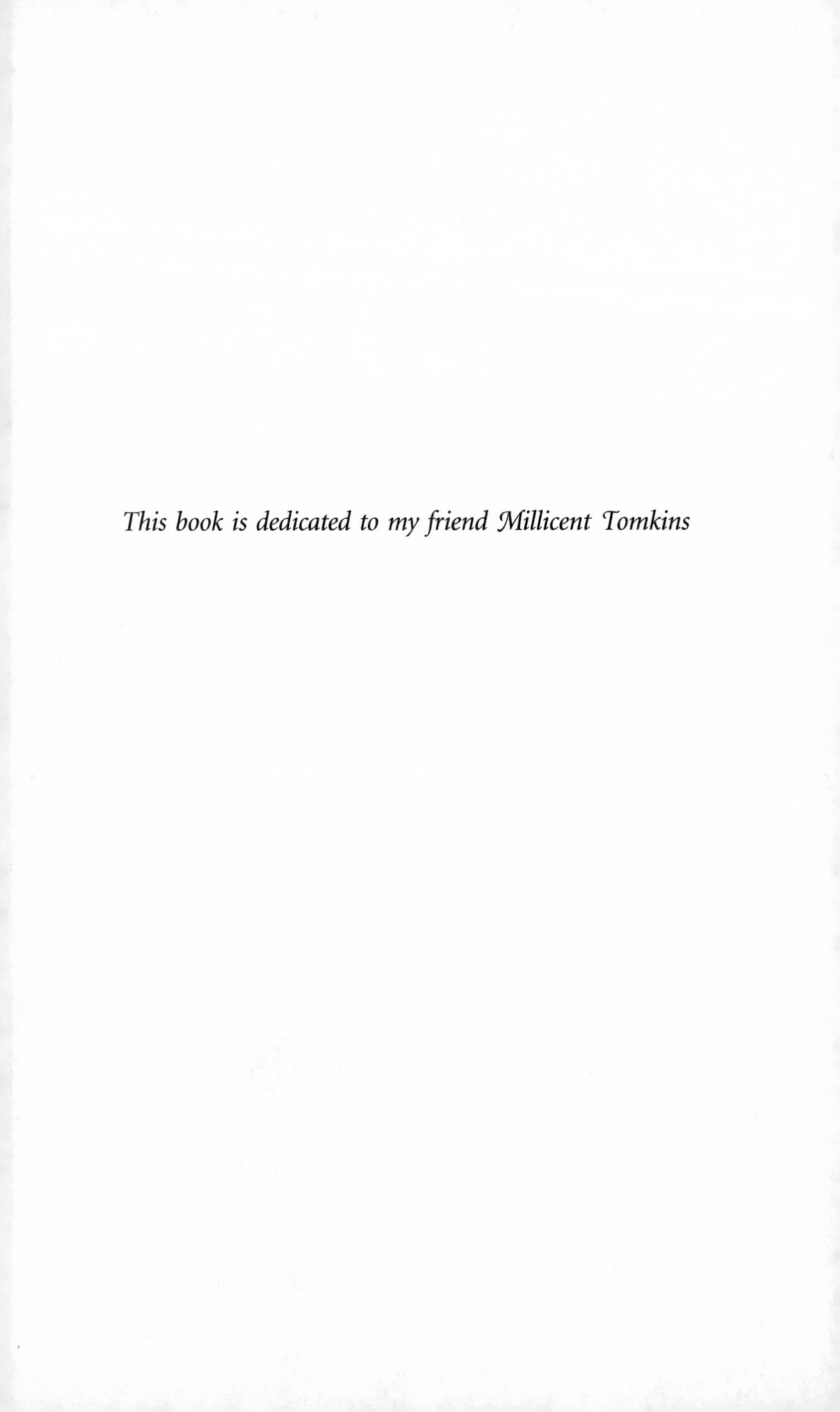

This book is dedicated to my friend Millicent Tomkins

1 THE BULLET

JENNY SAT in Horacio's living room with their dog, reading a book about Michelangelo, mostly studying the pictures. She didn't know where Horacio was, which was no big deal. After eight years together, the two of them didn't particularly keep track of each other's coming and going. She was fresh from a shower and wore a light blue sweatsuit. Her short dark hair was still damp and clung to the fine bones of her head, more like gleaming feathers or fur than hair.

The Mill Valley house was a huge sprawling structure that Horacio worked on when he wasn't building mansions for other people. It straddled the ridge opposite Jenny's own little dragonfly of a house, which she used as a studio or, sometimes, when she needed to be solitary, as a refuge.

She sat before the fieldstone fireplace, which was big enough to roast an ox. The little fire she'd set was lost in the cavern of rocks, flickering forlornly. Jenny thought there should be Irish wolfhounds lying in front of it instead of Abraham, a German short-haired pointer, which was a normal-sized big dog. The living room itself was of an immensity that Jenny felt required suits of armor and medieval tapestries to do it proud. Still, she was always able to make herself cozy—given a chair, a lamp, a book, a bit of fire.

It was around midnight when she heard the key in the lock. "Hi, honey, I'm home." He often hailed her with the classic phrase because they were such an un-classic couple.

"Hi, honey," she replied, briefly looking up from her book. "I'm home, too."

"Call the vet, will you? Tell him to come right away." Abraham, lying at her feet, greeted his master with the same amount of excitement she had, a lifting of the eyelids. Why call a vet? she wondered. Abraham was in splendid health. He hadn't been in a serious fight for six months. It mystified her how a dog so seemingly peaceful could periodically do so much damage to himself, but he was a lot like his master: highly sexual, with a wild, lawless streak. What looked like calm, even laziness, was really banked force.

"Vet?" she inquired.

Horacio walked slowly into the room and lay down on the couch. "I've been shot." The front of his shirt was covered with blood.

"Oh, my God! Horacio!" Jenny leapt to her feet with alarm, dropping the book on Abraham. "Sweetheart!" She knelt by the couch, looking at his pale perspiring face rather than the blood, which might cause her to faint. "Let me drive you to the emergency room. You should have gone straight there."

"No hospital, hon. They'd have to report it to the police. The vet will do fine. He owes me one."

Jenny remembered that Horacio had set the man up in business. Then, suddenly, she doubted her lover, remembered what a joker he was and how she always got taken in by him. He was a good actor and this gory display was typical of the sort of melodrama he rejoiced in. It occurred to her to dip a finger in the sopping shirt and taste it, see if it was ketchup or, knowing him, *salsa picante*. If she looked closely there might be bits of jalapeño pepper in the "blood." It amused him to no end to play her for a fool.

But if she might faint from looking at the blood, what might she do from tasting it? Have a cardiac arrest?

"Jenny, save me," he moaned. Yes, this was a prime example of one of his mock predicaments enacted purely to frighten her.

Meanwhile Abraham had lumbered over and was whining, a new sound in his slim vocal repertoire, which didn't even include a full-blown bark. Unlike Jenny, he never fell for Horacio's jokes. She decided to trust in Abraham and his unprecedented sign of concern. She would forego tasting the blood and believe in it.

"Abraham, you call the vet," Horacio suggested in a faltering voice. "Jenny doesn't love me anymore. She wants me to die. I've gotten too old for her. Too gray. I can't get it up anymore."

"You never were reliable about getting it up." She spoke over her shoulder, on the way to the phone. She roused the animal doctor, related the circumstances, and he said he was on his way.

She covered Horacio with an afghan. He was beginning to shake. "Damn it, you're in shock. You should have an IV. You should have proper care. I hate this vet idea."

"A bullet's a bullet whether it's in an animal or a human. We're not talking about some baffling disease that needs to be diagnosed."

Jenny remembered that his body had hosted bullets before. Once he had shot off his ear. He groaned. Empathetically, Abraham groaned too.

"Good dog." This was high praise from Horacio, who didn't believe in talking to animals, let alone complimenting them. Neither he nor Abraham was acting normal.

Jenny wet a towel and tenderly wiped the sweat from his face which, normally ruddy, was now quite gray. "Tell me what happened."

"I was in a liquor store that got robbed. I got caught in the middle of it."

Wherever he found people in trouble, he lent them a hand, whether it was car trouble, or a lost child, or a beggar needing money or work: things and people Jenny never even noticed. Horacio could find trouble on an empty street.

"I bet you were playing the hero. You tried to protect the cashier, didn't you?" Horacio closed his eyes, slipping out of consciousness.

With shaking hands she gently pressed the towel over the wound, stanching it. She closed her eyes, fighting back tears until, the next thing she knew, the vet was taking her place at Horacio's side.

In the morning when Jenny went to the door to get the newspaper and read about Horacio's escapade, it wasn't on the porch. Could Horacio have dragged himself from bed, wheeling the IV along with him, gotten the paper and hidden it?

If he had hidden it, it was because he had lied and, come to think of it, what was he doing in a liquor store when he didn't drink to speak of, didn't smoke or eat candy bars? He couldn't have been getting a six-pack for his men at that time of night. They wouldn't be working construction that late and in any case they were the ones who ran errands for him.

Where would he hide it? She went to the pile of old papers by the fireplace and found it wedged in the middle of the stack, spotting its white edge among the tan and yellow.

No report of a liquor store holdup, but there was an item about a Pacific Heights resident who had taken a shot at a fleeing jewel thief. "I warned him first but he didn't stop. I think I winged him but he still didn't stop," the paper quoted.

Jenny's blood ran cold.

She went to look in his new Mercedes convertible, but there was no sign of any jewels. His old Porsche, now up on blocks, had a secret compartment, but she didn't know if the new car did. He had a statue of a wooden soldier that he hid things in but that was in his bedroom. Never mind, she didn't need any proof; she knew Horacio had been the fleeing burglar.

Jenny let Horacio's wound heal before she confronted him. The evening of his first day back at work she baked him a chicken dinner in a clay pot, one of his favorites. As she arranged the carrots, potatoes, and onions around his half chicken, he went to get a bottle of wine, making a celebration of his being up and about, which was too bad since she'd vowed to herself to have it out with him and it was always a shame to have a celebration turn ugly.

She swallowed her words until dinner was done but she'd swallowed them for so long, almost ten days, that she felt sick to her stomach and could hardly eat.

As he got up to clear the plates she said, "Horacio, wait. I have something serious I want to say."

He sat down again, fixing her with his hazel eyes. His face looked kindly, vulnerable, and interested. He was all those things but she knew he could make his face look any way he wanted at any time, that it did not necessarily express his current feelings or state of mind. It was a handsome face, too. When she first met him it was almost boringly handsome, but the years had patterned lines of character.

Jenny folded her arms on the table top. "When we decided to live together, the understanding was that you would give up your thieving. Before, when we were just friends, I didn't want to meddle in your life and affairs, but I told you that if I was going to love you and live with you, I wanted you to be honest and, of course, I wanted you safe. You said you would go along with it and I believed you."

His expression gradually faded—first the interest, then the openness, then the kindliness. Still, he listened and looked at her. He didn't get up and leave.

"When I read in the paper about the burglar that had been shot, and nothing about a liquor store holdup, I realized you were back in the game. I don't know how long it has been that you have lived this lie but I know that I can't trust you anymore.

"I love you with all my heart. You know that I do. But I can't live with a criminal. I have to be true to myself and my beliefs, true to my art. Even if I weren't a stickler for living honestly, from now on, every time you were late home I'd be thinking you were at it again and that your life or your freedom was in danger. I can't handle it. So I'm leaving you, Horacio." Her voice cracked. Up until then she'd done well.

He reached a hand across the table to her. "Don't go, hon."

She didn't take it, only folded her own arms closer to her breast. "I really thought you knew," he said. "There have been a lot of late nights over the years. Didn't you wonder?"

"No, because I completely trusted you." She flushed with anger at his betrayal. With the rehearsed statement out of the way, she could begin to express her ten days' worth of churning feelings. She had thought Horacio only played her for a fool sometimes, for fun, for a joke, but in fact he'd been constantly deceiving her for years. "Horacio, there was no reason. You make plenty of money as a contractor. And you have all the money Uncle Arthur left you."

"It isn't money. It's never been money. It's the feeling of being alive, on the edge. Life is so boring otherwise and I've never once felt more dishonest than the next guy. You're unusual. You are an honest person. But no one else is; you just can't see it."

"No, no, I'm not honest. I've lied, dissimulated, and I've done worse than that, worse than anything you've done, I've . . ."

Jenny couldn't say the word but Horacio knew what she was thinking about. She'd killed someone. Maybe. Maybe her blow wasn't the death blow. She'd never know. But . . . well, she wouldn't drag that all up now.

She sighed. "Anyhow . . . I try to be honest. But you are a truly kind person, Horacio, a better person than me in your benevolence to others, but . . ."

"I need the excitement, Jenny. After all, I don't even have the fun of fooling around with other women. I have to be faithful to you."

Jenny knew Horacio was purposely getting her off the track but she succumbed. "You don't have to be faithful to me," she said, even though the thought of him with someone else was like a knife turning in her heart. "I wouldn't want you to have to be, you must want to be."

"Are you kidding? No man wants to be!"

"Don't you remember how you hated it when you were saddled with all those women in love with you, driving you nuts, and half of them having babies by you?" Three different women had provided Horacio with four children, all of whom he supported.

Sadly, Jenny had not become pregnant by Horacio, but she was fond of his children, especially his African-American daughter Mae, who she had guided over the treacherous teen years to college. Mae would be very upset by her leaving Horacio but Jenny couldn't think of that now.

"Anyway, now there's AIDS. You're lucky you had to be faithful." Jenny couldn't seem to get away from the fidelity question and back to the honesty issue. Her mind flailed. If she left him he undoubtedly was going to be with other women. Was she going to be able to handle the loneliness and loss, the jealousy?

It was better than the alternative. She had her little house, her work. She would survive. "It's too bad," she said bitterly, "that I was so boring to live with you had to return to criminality to amuse yourself."

"Jenny, I never stopped being a thief. Just like you could never stop being an artist. It's ingrained. It's who I am. And yes, you are boring to live with."

Jenny smiled. It was true. She was no ball of fire.

"Still, you're the only woman I have ever lived with and it's been wonderful. I love you."

"I love you too, Horacio." She turned her face away to hide the gathering tears.

"But you're still going to leave?"

"Yes, I am."

"Even though all these years we've been together I've been a thief and you didn't know and it was fine?"

"Now that I know, it wouldn't be fine any longer. I wouldn't respect you. I would be constantly afraid for you. And I would be living on tainted money, which is unacceptable."

"What money are you going to live on?"

"I'll start selling my paintings."

For once he was unable to hide his expression, which Jenny read as, "That'll be the day." Not because he didn't admire her art—he did—but she knew he couldn't imagine her putting it on the market or anyone paying much money for her particular subject matter—rocks—no matter how beautifully rendered.

She stood up from the table, began walking away, wavered uncertainly, feeling more should be said at the end of a long, stable, loving relationship, but then she kept walking, and before she knew it, she was out of the room, the house, their life together.

2 SURPRISE BEQUEST

A YEAR OR SO LATER, on a quiet street in Mill Valley, the alarm clock startled Jeff Haymaster awake. For the first time he didn't sit up and bump his head on the van roof. It had taken him a month to retrain himself from a lifetime of sitting up when the alarm went off. He didn't know if that was a short time or a long time. How long would it take other people? Maybe other people didn't immediately sit up the second the alarm went off. As a boy he trained himself to do so, knowing that otherwise he'd fall back to sleep and be in big trouble with his mother, teachers and, in due course, employers. Was it the head bumping itself that pounded the message into his thick skull not to sit up? How long did it take Pavlov's dogs to learn that the ringing bell signified food? A couple of days at the most, maybe hours. But that was positive reinforcement. Although not getting one's head bumped was fairly positive too, in a negative kind of way.

Jeff hated living in a van. As he scootched down and off the bed and crouched over the Coleman two-burner to make breakfast, he proclaimed himself fed up with the situation. Awakening-retrained or not, he couldn't stand living like this another day. He was going to find a house to stay in even if it meant selling his soul, although his soul was fairly nonexistent and he wouldn't get much for it. He couldn't afford even a small apartment on his crummy salary, so far had he fallen in his career.

He'd gone from being a photographer on the *Chicago Tribune* to a catch-as-catch-can photographer for the *Mill Valley News*, a giveaway with a circulation of ten thousand. And he didn't even have drink, drugs, or decrepit old age to blame for his fall. If anything it was athleticism. A mountain bike fanatic, he'd been determined to come to the hub of the sport, Mount Tamalpais in Marin County, hoping to get a job with the *San Francisco Chronicle*, but they weren't hiring—they were firing. So was every other newspaper around the Bay Area.

While waiting for the water to boil, still in his Quasimodo crouch, Jeff pulled on jeans, T-shirt, and sweater, then poured the water over coffee and filter into his mug, putting three eggs into the remaining water. Over the other burner he toasted bread on a fork. Five minutes later he scooped the boiled eggs from their shells onto the toast and opened the door so he could sit half in, half out. He ate his breakfast eagerly, polishing it off with a quart of milk. He tried not to let the meal be spoiled by the glares of two women walking their dogs, or by the twitching curtain from the window of the house in front of which he was parked.

It was a nice morning. With food in his belly, he cheered up. It was early March and the plum trees all over town were in knockdown, drag-out bloom. Back home there was a blizzard and sub zero temps. What did he have to complain about? He was lucky. This was what he wanted. He didn't miss the big city excitement, danger, or stimulation. He liked this little town and the mountain it was built around. He only wanted a home he could stand up in.

As for his job, at least he had a darkroom at his disposal. He might have knocked together a photographic essay of some sort, except he seemed to have lost all ambition. Maybe he could use his killer looks to some good effect, he thought, being only somewhat ironic. His body would fetch more than his soul. At twenty-eight, it was hard as a rock if a little on the short side. When he bothered, women toppled like ninepins before his laser-green glance. His personality? He was good to his friends, but even they admitted to his having a mean streak if he didn't get his way—only apparent in California, this mean streak. In Chicago they would admiringly call it being a go-getter. In California you didn't go-get, you let-come. That was all right. He could tame himself. He could relax, even if it meant gritting his teeth to do so.

He'd peaked too early. Where can you go from winning the Pulitzer Prize at twenty-three? Over the next five years he'd burned himself out, lost his lust for work, and so, once here, finding no good jobs available, he was willing to accept the low-powered job at the *News.*

All he wanted to do was bike, place his wheels on the mountain trails and see how fast he could turn them. There were two groups of bikers, those who wanted to amiably share the trails with the hikers and runners and those who wanted to terrorize the hikers and runners off the trails. The second group were his kind of guys. Fuck the hikers. The bikers were banned from the hundreds of miles of slender, twisting mountain paths—the single tracks that were the most fun to ride. They were asked to keep to the fire roads, the stodgy old railroad grades, and the wider open trails of the headlands. But some of the bikers were secretly slashing their own mountain trails to feel the thrill of the narrow downward plunge. Hikers had responded with tacks on the trails. Great. This was war!

Jeff cleaned the van's interior. Then he drove to another neighborhood so he wouldn't get reported for vagrancy. These people didn't like strangers driving through their streets, let alone parking on one and spending the night. Eating breakfast at the curb was a hanging matter.

One difficulty was that the town was built on hills and in canyons so there weren't many level streets with curbs to park at. It was all narrow curving roads with driveways. His options were limited. But he found a place on a street he hadn't frequented for a week or so, then took his bike from the roof and pedaled to the newspaper office on Miller Avenue to see what champion potholder-maker, little league team, or doddering dahlia grower they would want him to photograph today.

The editor gave the address of Jenny Hunt, on Hillside. "Try to get her with a big smile on her face," he said. "She ought to be happy. We got a tip that she inherited a million dollars. The money's from a living trust, so no probate and no taxes—and it's not public. Can you imagine? A million bucks, tax free!"

Jeff usually didn't bother reading the story but this one was interesting. "SURPRISE BEQUEST TO STRUGGLING ARTIST," was the lead.

"Horacio Huntington, a local builder, who committed suicide by jumping off the Golden Gate Bridge on Valentine's Day, has bequeathed a million dollars to Jenny Hunt of this town as a grant with which to continue her painting. Friends say that he admired her art and felt she hadn't received the recognition she deserved. In shock at the death of her friend and seemingly unable to grasp the fact of the bonanza that has befallen her, Ms. Hunt was unavailable for an interview."

"I hear she's something of a shrinking violet," said the editor, who was fond of outdated expressions. He was a sweet old man, unlike any editor Jeff had ever known. "Try to be gentle."

"Gentle's my middle name. Do you know how old she is?"

"No."

Jeff hoped a shrinking violet would be under thirty. Trouble was, a violet with a million dollars wasn't going to stand around shrinking for long.

3 LOST IN SPACE

JENNY PAINTED in the studio of her house, which poised like a hang glider on the edge of a hill. The house, when it was built twenty years before, looked like a fragile architectural marvel that might take wing at any moment. Now, with the passage of time and too little upkeep, it looked flimsy and rickety, as if it might collapse into pickup sticks in the next stiff wind.

Jenny was working on a large oil painting with a small brush. She looked like a woman completely at peace. Observing her, no one would guess that her life was in a tumult. At the moment she didn't know it herself because, in her blissful creative absorption, she was able to forget.

There was only the infinitesimal sound of brush on canvas, almost a non-sound, but even if there were other noises, she wouldn't have heard them. So deep in her mind was she that it could be likened to a state of sensual deprivation. Her hand moved to the vision in her mind, duplicating it. She smiled as her brush slowly revealed a spool of thread with a needle in it. The thread was green cotton and had a sheen to it.

Over the years, Jenny had painted found objects—primarily rocks, arranged on a table, on a draped cloth—the traditional still-life, only with untraditional objects. No fruit, no wine bottle, no flowers.

One year she relinquished the cloth, and the objects on the table assumed the look of an alien landscape. The rocks could be boulders, even mountains. They cast long shadows across the canvas from a mysterious light source.

In time she relinquished the table and allowed the rocks to float on the white canvas, shadowless, just a few of them, arranged in space. In recent years there appeared other objects: a piece of sea glass, a shell, pine cones, a small fruit such as a grape or cherry so that her private cosmos was embellished with color.

Most recently she'd conceived the idea of putting her objects in actual space, as constellations, or planets spinning around a sun. A band of midnight blue at the top of the canvas grew ever paler and then white. That constituted the background.

The sun, shining from the right hand corner, was a corn muffin.

The spool of thread with the needle tucked in would be Earth. Faraway Pluto was a tiny apricot-colored snail shell. She hadn't decided about the others but she thought that Mercury, half the size of earth and closest to the sun, should be a paper clip. Mars might be a chili pepper since it was the red planet. Perhaps she could paint Mercury as a feather to symbolize the god with wings on his heels, if that wasn't too hokey. It would be awfully easy to get hokey with this concept. Anyhow, even if the painting didn't work, it was a breakthrough for her, using everyday tokens and bright colors, getting well away from the muted rocks, which had always been emotionally fraught for her, even before she'd killed someone with one.

Well into her third hour at the easel, Jenny painted and smiled until a loud knocking at the front door returned her to earth, to the needle and thread of her life.

It occurred to her not to answer, but she saw that it was past the time she usually quit for lunch, so she put down her brush and wandered out of the studio, through the living room to the front door. Opening it, she confronted a stranger and gazed at him in wonder since no one ever came to her door except friends or family. There were so many steps from street to house, they looked unconquerable to salesmen or religious maniacs. This man looked like neither. He looked like one of the nouveau swarm of virile young bikers who had taken over her lovely mountain in the last year, descending from who knew where, an alien race, not Big Foot but Big Leg, come to wreak havoc with meandering hikers such as herself. She had no animosity toward them, or anyone, only thought it was disturbing. However, she was captured by this man's green eyes, the very green she had attempted to create for thread-spool Earth. They were full of the most marvelous light. If she could just get that steady, burning green light on canvas, wouldn't that be something?

4 PIECE OF CAKE

JEFF THOUGHT that the woman who opened the door was pretty and just out of her twenties, no older. Her hair was short, dark, and glossy in an unstylish bowl cut which she probably did herself. Her eyes were large and dazed-looking; he hoped the expression wasn't permanent. He couldn't live with a woman who looked like she'd been knocked on the head. Her body, although long and thin, was still shorter than his own—a prerequisite with him. She wore black tights and a large blue denim shirt. Hard to tell about her breasts and ass. He'd hope to be happily surprised, but it wasn't that important, was it? She had a house he could stand up in and a million dollars.

"Yes?"

"My name's Jeff Haymaster. I'm sorry to disturb you. Did I wake you up?"

"No."

"I saw your car in the garage so . . ."

"I'm afraid it hasn't run for years. It's an Alfa Romeo Spider—a great car, but it's sixteen years old now and I can't afford the upkeep. The parts . . ."

Jeff wanted to assure her that with her friend dead she could afford the upkeep, but maybe that wouldn't be being gentle.

"Do you want to buy it?"

"No, I only mentioned the car because I thought it was a sign you were home. That's why I knocked."

"Well, yes, I am home, even though it wasn't a reliable sign. Not at all."

Jeff wished he could start all over again. He felt like he might be beginning to look as dazed as she did. She looked less ga-ga now, as if the talk had clarified her mind even as it served to confuse his. He hated the feeling of not moving forward in a conversation.

"I've been painting for hours," she explained. "I always have a little reentry problem. What was it you wanted?"

"I've come to take your picture for the *Mill Valley News.*"

"Why?"

Jeff took a clever tack. "I thought maybe I could get a picture of you with one of your paintings."

"I'm sorry, but . . ." She was still standing at the door and he was still on the stoop. He decided to step inside, passing her by, striding into the living room where a wall of glass overlooked Mount Tamalpais.

"A hell of a view," he said. "What a great house." He saw that there was a little level land beyond the window before it sloped down the hill. Room enough for a pool and Jacuzzi, although perhaps it was too soon to suggest it. He didn't want to be premature. He'd wait until he moved in, in a few days. "Do you live alone?" He looked around. The furniture, once nice, now looked shabby, though the rugs were the kind that got better looking as they aged. She must have had money at one time. Maybe a marriage went sour. With her old, inert car and her rundown house she had to be damned happy about the million. Time for her to stop mooning around.

A door at the far end opened onto a bedroom. The living room flowed to a dining room, then turned a corner into the kitchen. There was another door, this one closed. Over the river-rock fireplace was a portrait of a World War II flyer who looked like Jenny. That was the only picture.

She didn't answer his question, but looked surprised and helpless that he was standing in her house while she still stood at the door, as if she was the visitor.

The telephone rang on the table near the door. She ignored it, although he gestured and said, "Feel free," giving her permission to answer the phone in her own house.

A woman's voice came on the machine. "Jenny! It's Sal. I just heard about the money. That's great. I didn't know Horacio was so rich. Did you? Anyhow I'm thrilled for you. Hope you'll still speak to me. Bye."

Jenny focused and frowned. "Can you believe that? I keep getting calls like that from my friends. It's insulting for them to suggest I'd drop them because I'm rich. What kind of person do they think I am?"

"Don't worry. They're just feeling a little insecure. The threat of change, or the balance of power in your relationship being altered." Jeff ran his hand through his thick black curls, drawing attention to them. He wore faded jeans and a plain T-shirt that did not boast of any far-flung travels or dashing athletic event. He prided himself on his modesty.

"Power?" Jenny pondered and looked interested. "I never even think about who has the power."

"Well, they think about it."

"Do you?"

"No, because I always have the power."

She laughed. "Good for you. I guess I don't think about it because I never have it."

Suddenly there was a groaning sound from the kitchen. Jeff scowled. The violet didn't live alone. Apparently she lived with someone gravely ill or in horrible pain. He was philosophical: maybe the person would die soon.

A brown dog appeared from around the corner. "Abraham, I was wondering where you were."

He didn't come over to her but sat down as if the few steps from the kitchen had exhausted him. Jenny went over and patted him, squatting by his side with, Jeff thought, commendable leg strength. "This is my friend Horacio's dog," she said. Abraham seemed to perk up at his master's name. "He's not in the bad shape he pretends. He's just depressed. It's hard to say how old he is. He wandered into Horacio's life and then stayed for ten or twelve years. They had an understanding between them that they wouldn't become dependent on each other but I think Abraham did. Horacio said their agreement was that he'd feed Abraham if Abraham would guard the house and keep off the furniture and Abraham said okay as long as Horacio would not expect him to wag his tail." Jenny's voice grew tremulous with this long speech and wavered to a stop. She wiped away an errant tear.

Jeff ignored the emotional manifestations. "He doesn't seem to be guarding your house, by the look of it."

"My house means nothing to him." She frowned, looking school-teacherish and further into her thirties. "Horacio was so mean to just up and leave him."

Jeff thought "up and leave" was a strange euphemism for suicide.

Jenny pressed her lips together as if she had more to say on the subject but wouldn't. Jeff wondered if she was really talking about herself—that Horacio was mean to up and leave her. Better get off the subject if he was to fulfill his assignment of getting a picture with a smile on her face. It wouldn't do for the public to think the money was unimportant to her; that would be un-American.

"So, how about the picture?"

"I feel a little shy about showing you my paintings," she admitted.

"Have you ever had a show?"

"No, but people seem to hear about them and sometimes come to my studio to buy one."

"Tell you what. Just go and get one that you like and I'll photograph it here in the living room. That way your studio can remain sacrosanct."

She looked pleased, probably because he'd used the word *sacrosanct.* Time to disclose the perfect teeth, lift the curtain of the upper lip. He smiled. "It will be great publicity for you. At least around town."

"All right."

She left Abraham and went to her studio. She was gone for five minutes. Jeff tried not to be restless. Whatever she brings out, I'll tell her it's wonderful, he vowed silently.

She brought out a canvas showing five floating rocks. "That's wonderful!" he said. She smiled warmly and he took the photograph. God, she was easy. "I love that painting." He kept snapping the shutter. "I love you, too. You're beautiful," he said from behind the camera. She kept smiling. "Those eyes! I'm falling into them."

As he was extracting the film and putting the camera away, he said, "I don't want to disturb you any longer, but could I come back another day and see some more of your work? I'll call first."

She considered this for an inordinate number of seconds. Jeff checked his impatience with difficulty, managing not to tap his foot or crack his knuckles. "All right. I guess so," she said, not showing any enthusiasm, but not being wary either, which was good.

"How about tomorrow?" He pressed his advantage, minuscule though it was.

"Uh . . . well, possibly. Call first and . . ."

"Great! 'Bye, Abraham," he called to the dog, moving to the door. "Cheer up!"

Before exiting, he turned suddenly and stepped over to Jenny. With a light touch he ran a finger down her cheek, fixing her with his green glance, trying for tenderness with all his might. "You cheer up, too." Watching her blush, he thought: *piece of cake.*

Jeff leapt agilely down the steps to where he had stashed his bike behind the garage that was a mausoleum for the dead Alfa, not turning to see if she was watching him.

5 HER LOST HORACIO

JENNY, not watching Jeff's departure, went to the kitchen to get herself a glass of water and some fruit to take back to the studio, already regretting the scene just past. He had found her in a vulnerable moment. But wasn't every moment vulnerable for her these days?

At the sink she glanced out the window and saw a foreign object about a hundred yards away on her familiar private landscape. It was a trailer. How did a trailer get there? There wasn't a driveway. And it was on private property, not part of her land but of the acres attached to the house down the road.

Dimly she remembered a Lot for Sale sign that had gone up a month or two ago then disappeared. She hadn't worried about it, knowing the lot to be impossible to build on unless the house was designed by an architect as adventurous as her own.

Someone must have bought it. She'd been so blue since Horacio's suicide that she hadn't noticed what was going on in her own front yard—or side yard, to be more accurate. She stepped out onto the flagstone patio off the kitchen and saw a man in the distance, clearing the thick tangle of manzanita, blackberry, huckleberry, and Scotch broom that covered the uncultivated parts of the mountain's foothills.

Jenny wished her personality allowed her to start screaming, to rant and rave and stomp around, to take a shotgun and shoot into the air and drive the man off. It really was too much that on top of everything else, her marvelous wild stretch of hill would be cleared, bulldozed, reshaped and formed so that some monster of a house could go up to the tune of electric saws, hammers and staple guns.

No one built small houses anymore—the land around here was too expensive to fritter away on cottages like hers.

Jenny sighed. What a shame. Her wonderful-seeming isolation was gone forever, which was almost as bad as her wonderful Horacio, the great love of her life, being gone forever to the outermost limits of nowhere, which was where she imagined after-death to be, somewhere out in space beyond the darkness of dead stars and the sheer blazing light of live ones. Maybe he was a star now, she thought, liking the idea, even though she knew it was childish. He had always loved the night.

At the end of a good day's work, Jenny brewed a pot of herb tea and took it to the armchair that faced the mountain so she could watch the clouds being kindled in the sunset out of sight to the west. This was a nightly custom, with or without friends, although in the good old monied days, she drank wine or champagne. She sipped the almost tasteless tea through her lips and with her eyes drank in the pale streaks of yellow that underlined the orange clouds. She thought about her lost Horacio. The monied days were here again but she didn't know if she could touch his million.

Horacio had always been a faller. He'd fallen from curbs, cliffs, trees. He had fallen from the beams of houses he was building, or from roofs, windows, or cornices of houses that he was burglarizing. Over the years he'd broken his back, collarbone, leg, arm, and innumerable ribs.

These were understandable accidents for one who spent most of his time high off the ground, although one or two of them could have been suicide attempts. The line was fuzzy because he was given to depression. That was why it was not impossible for Jenny to imagine he'd jumped from the bridge, fallen finally from a place too high to recover from. There might have been a moment of release and peace as he fell, floating in space like one of her rocks, feeling elation maybe, before he cannonballed into San Francisco Bay and broke his body to bits. Even then, if he was still conscious, knowing Horacio, he would have tried to swim, but pretty soon the cold would get him and he would sink forever down into the dark secluding water.

Horacio was a survivor. He was physically strong. His health was robust. He had an unflagging sense of humor that didn't allow himself to take even his despair too seriously.

Jenny thought back to the night of the bullet, the shot that had severed their relationship. She had lived with him starting when she was twenty-nine. Now she was thirty-eight and, if he had not killed himself, he'd soon be turning forty-five.

He had been smart, sexy, funny, and intriguing in that she never fully figured him out or understood him. He was always fun to live with except when he got depressed and then she would leave him alone, going to her own house to paint or to San Francisco to visit with her beloved grandmother, while he pretty much took to his bed.

As a young woman, she had been mentally unstable but with Horacio she had grown strong, confident, capable, and able to love. She still was no world-beater but she got along okay even after she left him.

When she first moved back into her house, they hadn't seen each other at all for a while, then they continued to see each other as friends and then inevitably as lovers. But Horacio chafed at the situation. If they were lovers, he wanted them to live together again. Jenny had said only if he would promise to live honestly and he had replied that he wasn't going to be dictated to. All this had been fairly recently.

"When you end up in jail or dead, you'll wish you'd agreed," Jenny said.

"I'd rather be dead than just a poor working stiff."

"Then don't work."

"What will I do? Sit around all day listening to you nag me?"

"I am not a nag, except about this subject."

But the fact was, the subject always came up and she always started nagging and she hated herself for it even more than he did.

One time she had tried to teach him one of her theories. "I have this theory, that you can change your character by punishing and chastising your hands and feet."

"Really?" Horacio had said politely.

"Yes. I got to thinking about the phrase 'Your left hand doesn't know what your right hand is doing.' And it got me thinking that your hands and feet do bad things out of habit that your mind doesn't know about or want to do."

"For instance?"

"Well, stealing. It's a hand and foot habit. I bet a lot of times you don't plan a heist. Your feet just take you there and your hands do the work. Or think of an alcoholic. He doesn't want to keep drinking but his feet take him to the store and his hands reach for the bottle and take it to the counter."

"So he should slap his own hands and step on his own toes, chastising them all the while?"

"Exactly!"

"If that doesn't beat all. The great minds of the world would be surprised by your theory."

"Because great minds are all in their minds, not their bodies, so they blame abnormal behavior on the mind and psyche. It takes a simple mind like mine to realize our troubles are all in the hands and feet."

"What about the phrase 'Cutting off your nose to spite your face?'"

"That has nothing to do with it."

"How about 'Biting the hand that feeds you?'"

"That's another person's hand, Horacio."

"But you could bite your own hand as part of the punishment."

"Oh, Horacio, now you're just making fun. Won't you even try my system?"

"In a word, no."

"I just want to help."

"I don't want help. I want to do many more 'heists' as you so charmingly and wrongly call them."

"Very well then. We won't discuss it any more and we won't be lovers. That's that. I really think it's over with us. We've just been dragging on with it out of habit and, well, out of love."

"If it's really over and you won't move back in with me, I'm putting the house on the market."

"You mean you think twenty rooms is too much for you? Twelve thousand square feet?"

"I built it for you."

"That's a lie. You had fifteen rooms done when I moved in and you just kept adding on more rooms because you didn't want to finish it. In a way," she had added begrudgingly, "it is your masterpiece. You'd think a master builder like yourself would be satisfied with . . . Oh, never mind."

"I won't take less than three million. And that money won't be tainted."

"Tainted money built it."

"See there you go again. I can't stand it. I actually am beginning to hate you. This is good-bye. You'll be sorry."

"I already am sorry. Sorry I ever met you." Horacio had slammed out the door. And that was her last sight of him—a month before he died. What a horrible ending. One time they'd been in Puerto Vallarta and they'd gone to the beach for a swim but there had been a storm the night before and the waves had swept away the piers, along with most of the beach itself. The waves were still dangerously high and Jenny had asked Horacio not to swim. They got into a fight about it and, naturally, he, not to be dictated to, marched off into the water while she, naturally, shouted after him, "I hope you drown!"

He almost had. Once out beyond the surf, he could not get back in. The waves were smashing into the sand and sucking him back. He hadn't had the strength to fight through. A crowd of people had gathered to watch, but no one helped. What could they have done? Only an insane person would plunge into such a churning maelstrom. Horacio had been tiring fast and it had been a lucky break that a particularly sinuous monster of a wave had lifted him up and thrown him down on the beach practically at Jenny's feet.

Later he had told her that he knew he was going to die and could only think that it was a stupid way to go.

She had told him how "I hope you drown!" kept ringing in her head and she knew it would ring there for the rest of her life. "And then of course I kept wondering about all the difficulty ahead—getting the body out of the country, dealing with the officials."

"You were worrying about Mexican bureaucracy while I was fighting for my life?"

"Of course I mostly was worrying about my hateful last words."

"Worrying about everything but me."

Now her last words, "I'm sorry I ever met you," were not necessarily ringing in her head but definitely preying on her mind. Sorry to meet Horacio who, aside from her painting, had given her the only happiness she had ever known?

Jenny's tea had gotten cold as the cloud colors folded into the oncoming darkness. The mountain turned black. A few stars appeared and she thought that stars didn't seem to twinkle like they used to, even if Horacio was one of them. She got up to turn on some lights and thought about fixing some supper, having finished with thoughts regarding her lost lover. Except for a tag-end thought, spoken aloud.

"I left Horacio to get away from his tainted money and now he has given it to me—as a final joke, a totally unfunny one. If so, where is he? Surely he'd stick around to see the joke played out."

6 THE TAINTED MILLION

JENNY WAS THROWN FOR A LOOP the next day when she collected her mail and saw her beaming countenance on the first page of the paper under the words, "Surprise Bequest to Struggling Artist."

"Oh no," she said aloud as she climbed the thirty steps back to her front door. "How disgusting."

Abraham, who'd spent the night away, appeared at her heels, and followed her up the stairs with small forays to snuffle in the weeds. It had rained and, in the pine needles and spider webs, drops hung shimmering in the morning sunlight.

"Abraham, look at this disgusting picture. I seem so thrilled that Horacio is dead. There are people who have known me all my life who have never seen me with a bigger smile on my face. I might as well have thrown him off the bridge myself to get his million, the way the picture looks."

Abraham looked sympathetic, then preceded her into the house and made a beeline for his water dish, which he lapped dry without splashing. Then he sat down by his food dish and waited. Jenny poured in kibble. While he crunched away, she moaned on.

"And my painting, which was to have been the main thrust of the photo, according to the wily photographer, is cropped to a fourth. I might as well be showing an empty canvas. You can barely see any content. There's just one, lone, pitiful rock looking meaningless without its companion rocks, and it doesn't appear to float or have any dimension. It looks like a splat, a bird-dropping. This photo is not going to send throngs of collectors to my door. Why did I ever agree to this?"

She went to the window and stared at the mountain thinking, what if Horacio were alive and saw this picture of me looking overjoyed at my surprise legacy? Surely it would occur to him to wonder why the money wasn't tainted anymore, and to wonder how his death purified it for Ms. Woman of Integrity.

She stood still, looked around, listened. She heard a chattering squirrel, an ailing refrigerator motor, Abraham's breathing. She couldn't shake this new feeling that Horacio wasn't dead, was maybe even watching her, watching her reaction to the windfall of magically purified money. It began last night when she'd got to thinking about how much he loved a good joke but she knew it was wishful thinking, based on no information, and was only making her grief harder to bear.

The truth was, she hadn't wanted the money. At first.

When she had first heard about it, her intention was to give it to his kids but when she mentioned this to the lawyer, it turned out Horacio had put plenty of money in trust for them.

"My second noble intention was to give it away. But to whom? How could I choose?"

Now she wasn't talking to the dog, she was on the telephone, talking it over with her grandmother who, in a way, was her closest friend, certainly her role model, although Jenny had yet to actually model herself after her.

"And then of course I thought about reserving a little, just enough to fix up the house and get a car and maybe some new clothes. Then, before I knew it, I'd spent enough of it in my mind to feel I'd better invest half of the rest of it for my old age."

"What about the other half of the rest of it?" Gram asked.

Jenny laughed. She pictured Gram, seventy-nine years old, dressed for the day (unlike herself, still in her bathrobe) probably hurrying off to some important board meeting one of the many she was invited to sit upon, but not sounding rushed, sounding interested.

"Well, it was tempting to think of traveling, or taking friends out to dinner now and then, or buying a bottle of wine when I felt like it—I'm so sick of tea—or just being able to pay for paint and canvas without having to eat rice and beans until the guy who sometimes buys a painting, shows up again."

"What guy is that, Jenny?"

Although Jenny had told Jeff Haymaster that people came to her studio to buy, only one person ever did. He would pay five thousand dollars for the larger oils, so if she sold one every three or four months, she could make it through the year. Barely.

"He's the agent for an anonymous collector but I'm worried that this collector could lose interest or die at any time."

"So much for giving the terrible tainted money away," Gram laughed, understanding, as she always did. "Poor Jenny. I had no idea you were in such straits when you left Horacio. I'm so used to thinking of you rolling in dough that the truth of your circumstances never struck me. Why didn't you ever come to me for help?"

"I didn't want to worry you, Gram. And I actually kept thinking I was pulling it off. At least I'm not in debt. There's that to be said."

"I'm going to come over and visit you. You always come to me in San Francisco. Now I know why. You didn't want me to see you in your derelict life. We need to have a good talk about all this. You need encouragement."

"Wonderful. Today?"

"I'll come tomorrow. I'll arrive in the afternoon and stay for the night, like you do when you come down here."

"I'll count on you to persuade me to accept my inheritance and not despise myself for doing so."

"I'm good at that sort of thing."

Jenny said good-bye and hung up. It was a comfort to think her friends would want her to keep the money. Although right now they might feel threatened by her good fortune, in time they'd be glad for her and glad for themselves for having a rich friend.

The fact was, she'd lived in the lap of luxury with Horacio. It wasn't until she left him that she learned how hard it was to survive on her own.

Because of her mental instability, she hadn't gone to college. Nor had she any secretarial skills. In the last year, she'd tried waitressing and clerking but she was terrible at both. She was too old and spoiled and dreamy. She wasn't a good worker, got summarily fired and now, with the economy the way it was, there weren't many jobs. She would be foolish not to keep the million. It wasn't really tainted. Death had laundered it clean. It wasn't a joke. It was a gift of love.

A thunderous knock on the door made her jump.

"Woof!" wheezed Abraham halfheartedly.

"Abraham, how wonderful! You've decided to guard the house."

She opened the door and there stood a stranger in a long brown coat.

Abraham, astonishingly, wagged his tail.

7 BRIGHTLY COLORED BATHROBE

JEFF HAYMASTER decided to go see Jenny without calling first. It was possible she was unhappy with the picture in the paper and wouldn't want to see him. Better to thrust himself upon her and let her lose all reason by the force of his dynamic presence. The plan for the day was to get physical, to clasp her in his arms. It wouldn't be a strain on his part. He found her attractive, sort of Audrey Hepburn-looking, a woman with a lot of style even in a big denim shirt: slim, graceful, big eyes, sweet smile. However, unlike Hepburn, she possessed a haunting sadness, even grimness, a look of having suffered unimaginable troubles. It could be age, or her current mourning, or being an artist. Whatever, it made her face interesting.

She was old, though. She had small wrinkles, rough-looking hands—a certain set-in-her-neuroses look that all women began to have once they reached twenty-five. Jeff considered all women to be neurotic to one degree or another and he wasn't patient with such behavior. Still, once installed in her house, he would make himself scarce. He wouldn't have to be around her that much. It was good she had her painting to occupy her.

And she didn't strike him as a woman who would want a lot of sex.

He stuck his bicycle behind her garage and started up the steps. As he rounded the big pine tree, he saw there was someone there before him, a man in a long brown coat.

Undeterred, Jeff bounded up the remaining steps. The door, on which the man had been knocking with a cane, was opened by Jenny. Abraham was standing beside her.

As Jeff appeared at his side, the man gave him a cold glance, turned back to Jenny and said, "Ah. I see you have company. I'll return at another time." He turned, roughly brushed by Jeff and descended the steps quite rapidly for a man with a cane.

"Horacio?" Jenny called after him. "Is it you?"

Horacio? wondered Jeff. That was the name of the man who died and left her the money. He didn't much like the idea of Jenny asking stray visitors if they were Horacio.

It was unsettling to see her shift from being dazed by her long hours of painting yesterday to being dazed at imagining she'd just seen Horacio today.

"Did you see that man?" Jenny asked him. Wearing a bulky bathrobe that was too brightly-colored and too long, she was not looking one bit like Audrey Hepburn.

"Yes."

"Describe him to me."

"Well he had the first coat I've seen in California and it was cashmere and probably set him back a couple of thousand dollars. He also had the first hat I've seen in California, a gray fedora. That and the Ferragamo shoes, probably cost him—"

"I'm not pricing him. I'm trying to identify him and I don't trust my own eyes. Tell me about his face and his body."

"It was hard to see either one with the coat and the hat and the beard. He had a light brown curly beard. I think he wore tinted glasses. He seemed heavy, carried a walking stick, so he might have a bad leg but from the way he took those steps, I doubt it. May I come in?" Man, it was hard to get through the door here.

"Horacio had a bad leg," she said, standing aside for him to enter—progress over yesterday, when he'd had to shoulder by her. "He limped some days."

"Yes, but Horacio Huntington is dead."

"The voice didn't sound like him."

"That's great."

"Horacio," she confided, "had a droning monotonous voice. It was distinctive. He always said he was going to do something about it. Maybe he did."

Jeff wondered what you could do about a droning voice. Take lilting lessons?

"I haven't seen him in the last two months—the month before he died and the last one."

"*Died* is the operational word here. A dead man's voice, of course, would be even more droning." Again she was leading him into a labyrinthine, not-forward-going conversation. He gritted his teeth. He was miles away from clasping her in his arms.

But then she laughed. As when she had laughed yesterday, he was surprised. It was such an outright merry laugh. She seemed to have a good sense of humor even in the midst of her troubles. The definition of a woman with a sense of humor, of course, was one who appreciated his own.

"Would you like some coffee?"

"Thanks."

Jenny poured two cups from a slim red thermos. She gave him a saucer too but he put it aside and perched on a stool while Jenny stood idly by.

"This morning I've been imagining Horacio lurking around."

Jeff told her he thought it might be part of the grieving process and she seemed interested and relieved.

"Horacio was always such a joker, you see."

"Faking a suicide would be a pretty mean joke."

"Well, I'd been rather mean to him the last year. Maybe I deserve a mean joke or two in return."

"Didn't they find the body?"

"No. Although they still could. His car was parked on the bridge. His wallet was in it, on the seat. The note said, 'Goodbye, dull world.' His affairs were all tidy. He was given to depression and had attempted suicide before."

"Sounds conclusive. I think you can be certain he's dead."

"Abraham sort of wagged his tail at that man."

"Maybe it was for me," Jeff suggested. "He saw me coming up the steps."

"Maybe it was," Jenny said, smiling.

Jeff thought it would be a good moment to embrace, except that she was holding her cup and saucer and had on that awful bathrobe. She probably had morning breath. He decided he wasn't up to it.

"Dogs love me," he said. Abraham farted.

Jenny looked at her watch. "Oh, dear. I have an appointment with a lawyer to go by Horacio's house. I've got to get ready. What a shame. I haven't had a chance to tell you how much I hated that picture you took of me."

"Do you need a ride?"

"I was going to walk. But a ride would save time, and I could tell you—"

"How much you hated the picture. Great. Go get ready, first. I can't look at that bathrobe another minute."

Jenny laughed. "You can't imagine how warm and snugly it is."

"Yes I can."

Jenny disappeared and Jeff walked into the living room, throwing himself down on the couch, taking possession. He liked this house. He closed his eyes, taking a catnap. When he opened them, Jenny was entering the room wearing a pale green wool suit with brown leather boots and matching shoulder bag. She wore a little makeup, not much, and her hair shone. It was a big improvement. First thing he'd do after he moved in was burn the bathrobe. Then they'd move on to more important matters like the swimming pool and weight room. He noticed a few buckets of water standing around from the rain last night and figured he'd allocate some of the money for the roof.

Jeff waited for her on the road, while she closed up the house. She trotted down the steps and looked askance at the bicycle. "This is my ride?"

He put his helmet on her head. "Climb on the bar here, side-saddle. You'll be fine." She did so. "Now relax. Lean against me. It's a matter of trust."

The ride started easy and ended hair-raising, since it was a twisting downhill road and, on principle, Jeff never used the brakes. They flew around the curves and swooped into town five minutes later.

When Jenny dismounted, she felt exhilarated. Jeff said, "Smile so I can see if there are any bugs in your teeth." Her color was high and her eyes shone.

"That was wonderful! Thanks!"

"How about dinner tonight?"

"Well . . ."

"At your house. I'll bring the food."

"I . . ."

"And I'll cook. See you." He turned the bike, reared it into the air, and pedaled away before she could say no.

She's a good sport, Jeff said to himself. This was high praise coming from him. To him the world was divided into good and bad sports and the good were outnumbered a hundred to one. Bad sports were anyone who made excuses, defended themselves, complained, whined, or refused to get on a bike because they were all dressed up.

She had defended her dreadful bathrobe but he was going to let that go. Other than that one small slip, she'd been perfect so far, and he had to admire the insouciance with which she wore the bathrobe at that hour of the day, thinking nothing of opening her door to strangers in it, thinking nothing of having coffee with a new (handsome, young, studly) acquaintance without apologizing for her appearance, or going and doing something about her appearance. She was pretty much batting a thousand.

Jeff had to remind himself that being a millionaire, she didn't need to bat a thousand. "A pretty, fairly young millionaire does not need to bat a thousand," he told himself. "You are looking for pleasant accommodations, not the woman of your dreams."

8 THE SECRET ROOM

THE LAWYER UNLOCKED HORACIO'S DOOR. This would be the last time she would step into this house, the one she had called Horacio's masterpiece. Although he had added on room after room to the main plan with haphazard abandon, the finished product had a surprising integrity, as if the final design was what the architect had planned all along. When she first moved in there were hallways going nowhere, stairs that bumped into ceilings, and doors that led to open space, often a drop of thirty feet—a house to get lost in, to get frightened in, but it had all come together into a proper mansion, or an improper one, stunning and beguiling. Jenny was there to see if there was anything she wanted to keep in memory of Horacio.

As promised he'd put the house on the market and it had sold quickly despite the real estate depression. He remained in residence up until his death and the escrow had closed a week ago.

He'd furnished the living room, dining room, game room (billiards and ping pong), master bedroom, study, and the four bedrooms for his children who spent the odd weekend, school vacation and month in the summer. The other nine rooms remained empty, except perhaps for the secret room. Did the new buyer even know about the secret room? Did anyone besides herself?

The children, or their mothers, had already put their names on the furniture, none of which Jenny wanted anyhow. Horacio's taste in furniture was like his taste in houses: big. Strange for a man of normal height. He liked the fortress feeling, she guessed, while she liked airiness, fragility, quirky design.

The lawyer, taking papers from his briefcase, made himself comfortable in a big armchair while she strolled about, seeing if there was anything that struck her fancy.

Horacio had collected colorful Mexican masks. His daughter Mae would like those, she bet. Mae was due to come by later.

There was a six foot high wooden British soldier, painted in shiny red, white, and black. It had a secret compartment in its body which Horacio used as a safe. Why not have the wooden soldier come stand guard at her door? That would be a treat. But how would she get it up the thirty steps?

Jeff could carry it. He was strong. Still under the sway of his animal magnetism, she was slightly reverberating from riding between his muscular arms, watching the pumping of his mighty thighs. Horacio, too, had been muscular, although not bulgingly so. His body had been smooth, supple, and sinewy, his hammer arm bigger than the other. His back had grown a little bent and his bum leg more bum. He had moved slowly, carefully, hating himself for having to, remembering when he had traversed high beams with élan and leapt from one high building to another without turning a hair. He would rather be dead than slowed down, she thought. In the bedroom she lay for a moment on the king-sized bed, reliving happy memories. Horacio would talk in his sleep, often about the price of redwood, and sometimes he would pretend to talk in his sleep, about other women, or about her, joking. Her eye traveled around the room then rested on the brick fireplace, on the brick that hid the control button for opening a passage to the secret room.

Suddenly, crazily, she felt convinced that Horacio was in that room, hiding out. He'd have a sleeping bag, a hot plate, maybe a mini refrigerator, and a small TV. He might have put in a small bathroom in advance or perhaps he would venture out to use the master bathroom when he was certain the house was empty. He wouldn't need to shave because he would have grown a curly brown beard. There would be some hooks on the wall on which to hang his beautiful long brown coat, his gray fedora. Galvanized, she sprang from the bed to the fireplace, removed the brick and pressed the button. She ran to where the wall was sliding open, slipping into itself. She stood tall, arms akimbo, prepared to say, "Ah ha!"

She was so sure he'd be there that when he wasn't, she burst into tears, and threw herself back down on the bed, this time on her stomach.

When her tears were spent, she felt like sleeping, a last sleep on Horacio's bed, their bed, a sweet sleep that might be a release, a forgetting, a conclusion somehow, but—something was bothering her. Before the tears had gushed to her eyes, veiling her vision, she'd seen something in that room, something she was so unprepared for that she hadn't registered it; her eye had not carried the message to her brain. When the vision of Horacio bending over his hot plate, emptying a can of beans, had not fulfilled itself, her mind was unprepared to accept whatever it was she did see. Her hopeful heart had been so crushed that she was unable to go forth, could not press on into the empty Horacio-deprived room.

What had she almost seen?

She got up, staggered a little, went to the opening of the secret room, and walked in. Seven paintings hung upon the walls. Her paintings. The ones purchased by the anonymous collector over the space of the last two years, providing her the money on which to live.

9 SO

SO," SHE WAS SAYING to her friend Sal over the telephone, after returning from Horacio's house, "you can imagine my feelings."

Sal was a professional, successful artist who painted huge canvases of people posed in strange tableaux. At first Sal had not taken Jenny's art seriously, finding her paintings merely amusing, but as the years passed and Sal saw how dedicated Jenny was, she seemed to change her mind. She began to appreciate what Jenny was doing and even compared her to the great Italian artist Morandi who just kept painting the same old jugs and jars and vessels in dusty pastellish tones until they began to attain a mythological majesty.

"Or maybe you can't imagine," Jenny continued. "I felt touched that Horacio had looked out for me, seeing I was unable to make it on my own, and also touched that he had hung my paintings where he could look at them. There was a table and chair in the room so I guess he spent time there. And you know, Sal, I'd never seen my paintings nicely hung, all in a room, a whole bunch together. They looked really good. I was impressed!"

"There you are," replied Sal. This last year she'd been leaning on Jenny to try to get a show but Jenny sensed that their friendship required that she not compete in the public arena; that even now, when Sal acknowledged her as an artist, it was only with the understanding that she stay reclusive, eccentric, unknown, like a little pet artist who would not be threatening, which was fine with Jenny. Jenny did not want to be a famous painter; she only wanted to paint.

"But the trouble is that I've been so thrilled to think there was a mystery collector who valued my work that I was bitterly disappointed to find out it was just Horacio, as usual."

It occurred to Jenny, suddenly and sorrowfully, that Sal's change of heart about her work corresponded with the fairly handsome prices paid by the mystery collector.

"How can anyone want to collect your work if they've never been able to see it?" Sal asked. "You seem to think they can learn about it through osmosis or something. But they can't. You have to put yourself out there."

"I'm still counting on osmosis."

"I can't much sympathize with your situation. Remember how you used to be afraid the mystery collector would lose interest or die? Well, he did die—but he left you a million dollars to go on with and, according to the paper today, it was because he admired your art. That's pretty nice. You can't ask for more than that."

Jenny couldn't go into the whole *sturm und drang* of not wanting to accept the million. Or that it would have been the mystery collector's money which would have allowed her not to accept it.

Jenny heard a knock. "Someone's at the door," she said. "Mae, I think. I'll talk to you later. 'Bye."

Horacio's daughter Mae hugged Jenny tightly, as if they'd been a long time apart. Now that Mae was in college, their get-togethers were rare, even though Berkeley was only fifteen miles away.

Like Jenny, Mae was grieving and, also like Jenny, her feelings about her father were in conflict. The conflict, because of her illegitimate birth, had been nourished by growing up with a mother who hated her father.

When Mae was fifteen, she'd run away from home to live with Horacio and Jenny. This caused her more anguish for seeming to choose white parents over black although she was really choosing love over resentment. She was as white as she was black but with all such children, her loyalty was to the black race. She was hard on herself and she got a hard time from her black friends, too, over her decision to live with the white parent.

Mae threw off her leather jacket and sprawled on the couch. She wore black jeans and a pink T-shirt and boasted a sharp new haircut. She had Horacio's chiseled features and hazel eyes but her skin was dark.

"I saw the wooden soldier down the steps. Why did you choose that idiotic toy over all the other fine stuff?"

"Horacio loved it," Jenny said. "I do too. Look at those." She gestured at the canvasses which were stacked leaning against the wall, "My paintings. Horacio was my mystery collector."

"He was? Well, shit! How do you feel about that?"

"Surprised. Disappointed. Deeply touched."

"He's going to keep his old hooks into you from the grave. He's so controlling. Probably why he left you that mighty million, girl."

Mae didn't know about the taintedness angle, and of course didn't know about her father's thieving, but she knew Jenny was struggling about accepting the money. "Should I take it, Mae?" Although twenty years younger, Mae was wiser in the ways of the world than Jenny, and Jenny valued her advice.

"As long as you're doing what you want, not what he wants."

"How can a little squirt like you be so smart?"

"You're looking at a college girl now."

Jenny kissed her. "That's right. I'm so proud of you."

"Boy! Glad someone is."

"Still," Jenny mused, "another word for hooks is love. Horacio and I loved each other so much."

"I know that. So why'd you leave him, then? I keep wondering." Mae let the question hang. She jumped up and went to the kitchen to scrounge in the refrigerator. "This is pathetic," she shouted. "You better take that money just so you can get some food and drink in here." As if summoned, there was a knock at the door, which opened without waiting for a response, and revealed the photographer, bearing bundles.

"Oh, I'd forgotten all about dinner," said Jenny. "Mae, this is Jeff. Jeff, my daughter, Mae."

They greeted each other, Mae took the bundles to the kitchen, and Jenny asked Jeff if he would carry up the wooden soldier. "It's not as heavy as it looks."

He turned and went. Mae raised her brows and said, "Nice ass."

Jenny flushed and said she hadn't noticed.

"I bet." Mae rolled her eyes. "Who is he?"

"The guy who took my picture that was in the paper today. The one where I look happy Horacio died."

"Don't be so sensitive about everything."

"I keep wondering what Horacio would think if he saw it. I keep thinking he did see it."

"What do you mean by that?"

"All today I've been thinking he's still alive."

"Mom, he's dead and gone. Get a grip. We can still love him but we have to move along. Right?"

After Mae departed, Jeff asked Jenny about her. Jenny explained that Horacio wasn't black, although he was a little of everything else: white, Iroquois, Mexican. Mae was his daughter by a previous non-marriage but Jenny had mothered her through her teen years and they were close.

Jenny wasn't sure of her own blood. "I'm unusual in that I know who my father is but not my mother. I was left at my father's door in a basket."

"My mother is Jewish, my father's a WASP," said Jeff. "I get my square jaw from him. Jews always have round jaws."

"And your dark curly hair from your Mom?"

"Right, although these days she dyes her hair an awful red. I blame her for my height. You don't know how awful it is for a son to be shorter than his father."

Jenny laughed. "I can think of worse things."

"He'll always look down on me for being a Jew and for being short."

"Maybe you're smarter than he is."

"I'm not. I did have a triumph a few years ago but it didn't earn his respect. He said it was luck."

Jenny and Jeff were drinking wine at an almost competitive rate which could be the reason they were revealing all this personal information in such a rapid-fire fashion. They also felt cozy together but mostly they felt drunk.

Jenny felt elatedly drunk, floating, out-of-body.

Jeff made dinner as promised, nothing impressive, but nonetheless tasty; spaghetti with Paul Newman sauce, a cursory salad, sourdough bread, and two bottles of Beaujolais. Except for intimate friends, Jenny had never told anyone about being left in a basket. Now she went further. "My father committed suicide when I was a teenager. So I have always felt abandoned by people who were supposed to love me. Now Horacio."

"I won't abandon you," he said.

Jenny did not know how to respond to this surprise pledge. It seemed rude to say she didn't care if he did, that he was not a loved one and never would be. How had they gone from Mae's bloodlines to this?

The next thing she knew she was lying on the couch in his brawny arms, although a second ago they'd been on opposite sides of the table that was littered with bread-crumbs and wine-spill. He was kissing her lips. Now he was opening her shirt and kissing her breasts. She felt like she was on fast forward. If she wasn't careful, and didn't put a halt to this, then the next thing she knew his penis would be inside her while, mentally, she was still sitting at the table and wondering how to reply to his pushy pledge. This sudden lovemaking was also unduly pushy but she didn't seem to be doing anything about it except enjoying it a lot. It escalated her drunken happiness—which was no longer an out-of-body but a thoroughly in-body experience—putting a halt to which seemed out of the question, let the penis come when it may.

She felt hot, she felt wet, and it had been a long while . . .

Her breast swelled toward his lips and tongue. She twined her legs with his to bring him close to her, to feel him inflate against her.

Then sure enough, like magic, their clothes were mostly off, a rainbow-colored condom was on, they rolled onto the rug for greater mobility, and he had plunged inside her, shouting, and she was shouting back, not a conversation, not personal revelations, just noises that were enough to make old Abraham wake up and get to his feet as if ready to do anything necessary to bring peace back to the house.

Abraham observed the squirming bodies, possibly thinking a dog's way more efficient, then lay down again when the noises subsided, doing his combined yawn and whine which was a sigh of relief. By then, Jeff and Jenny were in an L-shaped position, on their sides, legs clasped, sort of a wrestling hold, their heads as far away from each other as heads can be when two people are connected in the middle.

Jenny disengaged herself and staggered to her feet. "I'm cold. I'll be right back."

"Not the bathrobe! Anything but the bathrobe!"

"Okay, let's go to bed."

"Excellent idea." He got up and accompanied her. "You know, I vowed this morning to embrace you today," Jeff paused because of her expression.

"Vowed? Really? How strange. It all seemed so spontaneous."

"It was," Jeff said hastily. Usually women weren't so sharp so soon after coitus. "I'd forgotten the vow. I just remembered it now."

Jenny wondered if he'd forgotten his more recent vow never to abandon her, because already that which had seemed unacceptable twenty minutes ago, now seemed crucial. It wasn't just that the sex was emotionally bonding—it was the orgasm. She hadn't had an orgasm with Horacio since she'd originally left him. She'd forgotten the unspeakable bliss.

10 NOT TO BE HASTY

JEFF HAD PURPOSELY HAD AN ORGASM earlier that same day with a girlfriend so as not to be too hasty with Jenny. It hadn't worked. Or rather, it had worked.

His intention had been to, along with the fervent embrace, dole out a few kisses in a restrained sort of way, just enough to make her eager to see him soon again. In that way it hadn't worked. She'd been too responsive. But it had worked because he did not plummet ahead with the pull of his own desire and he could hold off for her orgasm, which came explosively like a man's. It was good. It was exciting. He liked it. She was all right.

Now Jenny slept beside him. The bed was comfortable. There was a skylight above showing the requisite stars, half moon, a tree. It sure beat contemplating the van roof. Maybe he would get up and do the dishes, not that he needed to earn any points. Still, he liked things neat and he could tell that she did too. The house was casual, even cluttered in spots, but it was clean. Well, maybe not as clean as he'd like it, but it was important to keep a leash on his normally vigorous critical faculties. What the hell, they could hire a cleaning woman. They could do anything. He sensed in Jenny an ambivalence about the money. He'd have to help her over any problems she had about it. Then he could always relieve her of it.

Maybe because it had been so easy to attain Jenny's bed and board, he began to figure on going for more, the money itself, unattached. He didn't even care about money that much. All he wanted to do was ride. But the money would enable him to do that. His father wasn't a millionaire. That was reason enough—to be something Dad wasn't, and to have more than him.

But why did he care so much about his father's respect that he let his entire life be jerked around by trying to gain it? He was programmed, that was all. He couldn't help it. He was like the Manchurian Candidate.

Jeff got out of bed. He let Abraham out and watched him go thrashing off through the underbrush toward the lot next door where a light beamed blurrily from a small trailer.

He went into the kitchen and did the dishes. No dishwasher. Time Jenny moved into the nineties—or at least the seventies. No TV either, or VCR. He hoped there was a washer and dryer. He snooped around, opening doors until he found them. Before returning to bed he stepped outside to see if Abraham wanted in but the dog wasn't there. The light was off in the trailer. The moon was off too, covered by a cloud, so when he got back into bed there were just the stars and the tree. And Jenny.

11 HIKER AND BIKER

It was not unusual for Jenny to go off the deep end over a man, but it had been so long since she had done so, in the years before Horacio, that she'd forgotten the tendency.

She would fall into a passionate affair. In a week or ten days she would come to her senses and see that the man she had given herself to, body and soul, was somewhere in the range between inappropriate and lamentable. She would free herself from the entanglement and retreat back into her shell.

When she woke up next to Jeff, she practically swooned with delight. Not only was he aesthetically and sensually pleasing, he also seemed smart and funny. He appeared to like her painting and it was helpful to her at this time that he was pleased at the prospect of her million. He would teach her to be, and he would fend off any fortune hunters by virtue of his vivid, passionate presence. Who would dare to compete?

It did not occur to her that he might be a fortune hunter himself since he'd been sent to her by the local paper, not come on his own, and he didn't have the treacly, charming, sycophantic ways she imagined a fortune hunter would have. He was straightforward, even rough, in his speech and, if anything, seemed honest to a fault, at least with regard to her bathrobe.

A fortune hunter wouldn't take her on a hair-raising bicycle ride and force himself upon her for dinner, bringing canned food as his idea of cooking. And she didn't perceive his compliments as flattery because she believed them. So she was thrilled, even honored, to awaken beside this paragon of masculinity who seemed to appreciate her for who she was.

Also, she was starved for love. The few times during their separation that Horacio had lured her into bed, or she had lured him, had been unsatisfactory because of everything that was unresolved between them, and because of the anger and disappointment that constrained them both.

Jeff's tightly curled hair did not muss in the night. His lashes lay long and thick upon his cheek. A blue shadow of incoming beard highlighted the strong bones of his face. His body, unlike Horacio's, was pelted with hair, but luckily not on his shoulders or back, although nothing could diminish his beauty to her heightened senses, not even hair on his nose. Even the fact that he'd taken all the covers and twisted them about his body in an irrecoverable way did not dismay her. It was only another manifestation of his vigor and zest, his seize-the-day mentality which would naturally include seizing the quilts while seizing the night and the woman.

So that he wouldn't awaken to view a face ten years older than his, puffy and creased, crowned by snarls, Jenny crept from the bed to transform herself. After showering, she looked longingly at her baggy robe but put on a silk kimono instead, one that had been Gram's, featuring white cranes on a shimmery golden background.

When she heard Abraham scratching at the kitchen door and went to let him in, her ears were assaulted by a snarling chain saw wielded by a man in a nearby tree. This was only the beginning of her peace and quiet being shattered. Thank God her studio was on the other side of her house.

She didn't notice that the dishes were washed and the kitchen was spotless, because now she began to think about her painting. Yesterday had been a lost day. Whenever she went a day without painting she felt deprived, felt less of a person. But today there was nothing to do but paint. Later Gram would come. And, right now, as she stood here, spooning coffee, an Adonis lay upon her bed.

She wrote him a note:

> Dear Jeff,
> Thank you for the lovely evening. Help yourself to breakfast. Coffee's in the thermos. I am in my studio for the day. My grandmother is coming for dinner and the night so don't plan to move in until tomorrow.

But if she left him this note, he wouldn't get to see her in her kimono. She'd better go to the bedroom and tell him in person. Anyhow, she wanted to talk with him, hear his lively voice.

"Is that for me?" he said, coming up behind her, reading over her shoulder. She turned around and they embraced. He was dressed in bicycle clothes: black tights, black T-shirt. She was glad he didn't wear those frightful multicolored shirts with brand names emblazoned on them.

"I'm off to the mountain to see how many hikers I can knock off the trails."

"How brave of you," she said, backing away from him.

He reached for her but again she detached herself.

"That's just great. And be sure not to look at the trees or sky or listen to the birds. The wild iris is in bloom, but give it a miss. And who cares about the incredibly fragrant blue clouds of lilac? Burn rubber. Gouge the earth. Don't consider the poor old hiker with his unsteady step who walked these trails in the Indians' footsteps before the first mountain bike was ever even thought of!"

"It was here on Mount Tamalpais that the mountain bicycle was invented," Jeff pointed out. "Looks like we've got a Romeo and Juliet situation here, only instead of a Montague and a Capulet we have a hiker and a biker. A hiker in a gorgeous kimono, I might add."

"I'd rather you add that you'll respect the trails and keep off them."

Less than a day into my new relationship, thought Jenny, and I'm already dictating his actions, becoming a nag. But what is a woman to do when men behave indefensibly?

Jeff was weighing his freedom of action against the obvious benefits of knuckling under. But if he was to give in on this one little point of not knocking down tottering hikers, where would it end?

"Fuck you," he said.

Nicely. If anyone can say "fuck you" nicely he did, in a soft, sexy voice, into her ear followed by a kiss. Surprised, Jenny laughed. She felt, she guessed, relieved at his unexpected response which managed to bring her down from her high-horse and abruptly terminate their bitter exchange. The discussion, for now anyway, was shelved.

"Happy painting," he said, "I'll see you tomorrow, not tonight, if there really is a grandmother. It sounds fishy to me."

Jenny laughed again. "You'll meet her soon enough. I'd like to introduce her tonight, but since she's coming to help me with my grief over Horacio it would sort of take away the thrust of the evening to introduce her to my new lover."

"How does our being lovers mesh with your grief?" he asked.

"It helps a lot. Yesterday I was acting crazy, imagining Horacio was still around, maybe playing a joke on me. Now I'm okay."

"No one would fake a suicide as a joke," Jeff said, feeling exasperated with Jenny's confusion. "The only reason a man might fake his own death would be if someone was trying to kill him or if the law was after him. And he'd have to have plenty of money to disappear with. Horacio gave all his money away."

Jenny nodded. She knew the police could easily be after Horacio and that some of his ex-girlfriends might want to kill him, but if he were going to fake a suicide he would do it only to keep himself amused.

"Good-bye, dull world" might have meant it wasn't going to be so dull anymore because he was going to have the questionable fun of seeing her not spurn the million that had stunk to high heaven when he was alive and now seemingly smelled as sweet as May flowers with him dead—especially with a handsome young lover in the picture.

But she had promised herself not to think about Horacio or anyone else today. She was going to paint.

"You're right. He's dead and gone and you're helping me feel better about everything. I've been alone too much. I've been sad. Today I feel happy, like I've discovered a lost emotion." She kissed him. "Have a good ride."

"You really are beautiful in that kimono."

"Thanks!"

"I like you naked, too." He loosened the sash.

"I like you naked a lot." She pulled down his tights. Still standing in the kitchen, they made love to the music of the chain saw.

12 COATED ONE

As Jeff pulled his bicycle from the van in front of Jenny's house, the man in the long brown coat was just stepping from a big Lincoln onto the narrow strip of dirt that weaved along the woodsy hill and called itself a road.

"Hi, there," Jeff greeted him. "I wouldn't go up now if I were you. She's gone to her studio for the day."

"Fuck you," said the man.

Not nicely, or sexily, not humorously, but not coarsely either. It was said quietly, but with such an ominous undercurrent, Jeff thought, that the effect was worse than loud and vicious. Much worse. It was somehow terrifying. It raised the hairs on Jeff's neck and made him swallow hard, as if he had an entire apple caught in his throat. He began to sweat and his bowels squirmed—all from the two quiet words. Who was this guy? But when Jeff felt cowed, he tended to attack.

"Do you know what a jackass you look like in that coat and hat? Where do you think you are, Prague?"

The grumbling roar of the chain saw broke the silence. A limb parted from a tree, disturbed the air, then landed, sliding down the embankment, stopping just short of the road.

"I know exactly where I am," the man retorted easily. "As for apparel, what's with the shiny black tights? Matadors, you know, stuff them in front to look fully equipped as a man. You might consider a similar tactic so as not to arouse people's pity."

Jeff's usual ready wit was stunned and to let loose a string of oaths, even in Yiddish, he knew would be lame. So he laughed.

He could tell by the tightening of the bit of face apparent beyond the hat, beard, and glasses that the laugh was as good a rejoinder as any.

He should have left it at that, but Jeff was never one for half-measures. He pulled down his tights, showed his equipment, which was above reproach, waved good-bye with his cock, leapt on his bicycle and was gone.

Gone fast. Pedaling like a maniac. Feeling exposed at the back. Scared. Expecting anything from a poison dart to a bullet. It was like one of those testosterone-inducing freeway encounters where you give a driver the finger and he shoots you in the head.

Calming down, Jeff took the short steep trail that led to the fire road which roller-coastered along the ridge. He tried to duplicate the two words said so admirably by the coated one, but couldn't.

"Fuck you," he said aloud a dozen times. Nope. He guessed you had to really feel like killing someone if you were going to sound like you might. But what is he pissed off at me for? What did I do? Well, if the man is Horacio, what I did was spend the night with his girlfriend.

Now he was falling into Jenny's unsavory state of mind regarding her possibly un-dead lover.

He tried to recollect whether or not the scary *fuck you* had been said in a droning voice. He didn't think a monotone could have that chilling timbre to it. His own voice was colorfully toned, and had an actor's range. He could even sing. Jeff unleashed his voice and did so.

He hit the mountain trail well beyond the legal speed limit and rode like hell, not forgetting to remain diligently deaf to the bird songs, to keep a vigilant eye out for tottering hikers for side-swiping purposes and on no account to smell the flowers.

Harry Beck was not so much surprised by Jeff's fine cock and testicles as by his hairiness. There was no line where the pubic hair ended and the chest hair began. It was dark, thick, even shiny.

Recalling the image, he shook his head in wonder, then turned his thoughts to the work at hand. Maybe the bicyclist was right. He shouldn't try to see Jenny when she was lost in her work and uninterested in anything else. And not when he was being observed by the tree surgeon, who seemed to be doing more gawking than limb dismantling.

But he'd already come back once, and next time he might not find her home. He walked steadily up the thirty flagstone steps and arrived at the door, not breathless.

13 GALERIE LA VIGNE

AFTER A SHOWER, Jenny pulled on jeans, a turtleneck jersey and a sweatshirt. She economized by not using the furnace except when layers of clothes didn't do the job, and she never used it at night, when piled-on blankets always did the job. But maybe all of that was going to change. She would be able to fire up the furnace and prance around in a bikini if she wanted to.

The noise of the chain saw jumbled her thoughts. She prayed she wouldn't hear it from the studio and hastened away from the sound.

She was crossing from her bedroom, stepping over Abraham, through the living room to her studio door when the knock sounded. Now what? She ardently wished to ignore it.

And who would be so rude as to come without calling first? Besides Jeff, that is. She would have to speak to him about that. But if he was moving in she couldn't have rules about calling first; they would be pointless. She tried to remember how it had been decided so soon that he would move in. It was the same way he'd come to dinner—suggesting it airily, confirming it without her acceptance, before she could graciously frame a rejection, then barging his way in, carrying the crummy dinner.

The knock sounded again, wood on wood, and she remembered the man who came yesterday morning, saying he would return. It must be him, with his coat and hat and stick. If so, she was curious. She wheeled about, retraced her steps, and answered the door. He handed her a stiff white card which said he was Harry Beck, representing Galerie La Vigne in Paris, France, and introduced himself as the person so named.

She put the card in her back jeans pocket and listened while he explained that he was scouting talent while here on the coast and had read about her in the local paper as being an artist shamefully unrecognized. His curiosity was piqued and he longed to look at her work. Would she be so kind?

As much as she wanted to get to her constellation painting, she knew she would be a fool not to be so kind. Here was long-awaited osmosis finally at work. "Please come in." Jenny noticed that, today, Abraham ignored the visitor. No querying woof. Not even an eyelid lift for a quick once-over of the stranger. He snoozed on. Probably she had imagined yesterday's tail-wag and woof. Or maybe it had been for Jeff. She felt that Abraham approved of her happiness, and therefore of Jeff.

As for herself, now that she had heard Beck speak several sentences, she was convinced he wasn't Horacio whose poor paltry voice could never have the range of this man's, let alone carry off such a subtle, indefinable, foreign accent. Still, there was something irkingly familiar about him, maybe because he was Horacio's size and build.

The main thing, she counseled herself, is that he doesn't walk the walk or talk the talk, so forget it.

"The paintings are in here."

Jenny led the way to her studio. She unstacked the seven paintings she had taken from Horacio's secret room and stood them against the wall so Beck could view them. They were her best work. She also set out six others for his regard about which she'd been indecisive, about which she was wait-and-seeing before destroying, because she did not keep work she felt had failed. These thirteen paintings plus two at Gram's apartment and the ongoing Constellation which stood on the easel now, and which she felt in her gut was going to be her masterpiece, were her life work.

"That's it," she said to Beck who was bent down and peered at one after the other. "I've been painting hard for fourteen years and this is all I've got to show for it but some of them aren't half bad. I feel like I'm getting there."

"Hmmm." He was currently looking at a still life of a faded jean jacket on a table with a long-stemmed, lavender rose, one of her few non-rock paintings. The pale colors looked luminous in the morning light.

The jacket belonged to Rowley—a deaf and dumb lover she'd had ten years ago. Who knew where he was now and what he was doing? She would always feel tenderly toward him. Maybe she kept the painting out of sentiment. Maybe it wasn't that good. She tried to look at it critically, through her visitor's eyes. She'd painted it while visiting Arthur, now dead. Why did she lose everyone who mattered most to her? All she had left was Gram, and it was terrifying that she was almost eighty. The thought of Gram dying made her heart feel like it was in a vise. It was intolerable.

Jenny looked around her studio and all her work suddenly seemed meaningless to her. None of the paintings were any good, all kept solely for sentimental reasons to remind her of loved ones dead and gone.

She looked out the window, her eye caught by a bright flash of color, a red-winged blackbird. It was like a signal to her that life goes on and there was meaning to be found. There was love, even though it meant loss. There was sex, even though its sensation was fleeting. There was art, which endured if it was any good and sometimes, every hundredth day or so, she believed hers was.

Beck seemed to be trying to get her attention, hemming and hawing, so she turned from the window and rested her gaze on him. "Ms. Hunt," he said. "I am interested in your work. It is original and powerful. It makes a profound statement about the end of the century and the end of materialism as we know it."

Jenny wondered if he might be a nut.

"Your surface is superb and the rendering of the objects as good as any I've seen from this century without photocopying or digitalized mechanical transfer. And yet these rocks"—he gestured to the ones littering her studio—"are not the rocks we see on the canvas."

Beck paused for a response but Jenny had none. He continued, "This is neither realism nor surrealism—it is magic realism brought to the painter's medium. These are wild unapproachable rocks."

All rocks are wild, Jenny thought. There are no cultivated rocks. But she liked the idea of their being unapproachable. There was a time she didn't like to think of when she used rocks for protection, to fortify her crumbling mind and assuage her fears. It had been a flung rock, on target, that had finally released her from her mental illness years ago so she had a special feeling for and understanding of rocks. But magic realism rocks? She didn't think so.

Still, let him suppose.

"I feel excited at the idea of offering you a one-woman show in our gallery. But I must confer with my partner. Of course, you have slides I can take away with me."

She looked closely at his beard. It was so curly it blurred the rest of his features. She was tempted to give it a tug but had the presence of mind to realize she would blow her chance of a show if she did. Instead she said, "May I take your hat?"

He looked nonplussed, then ignored her question and asked again, "Have you never taken slides of your paintings to send around to different galleries?"

She moved closer to him. Did he smell like Horacio? Hard to tell through the overlay of cologne. Horacio sometimes wore a scented antiperspirant, nothing like this subtle expensive scent. She dragged her mind to the subject at hand, knowing she was being impolite. Also, the man seemed so eager, it was touching. "I never felt ready for a show," she answered him.

"Believe me, you are ready."

"I do like the idea of it being far away in Paris."

"Who would not crave a show in Paris?"

“I have a photographer friend. He could take slides tomorrow.”

“Excellent. I will return for them that evening. You have only to give me the film, which I will messenger to Paris. I’m sure we will make a decision by the end of the week.”

“And I’ll have my decision for you by then.”

“I beg your pardon?”

“Well, I have to be sure I want to do this.”

“Young lady, there are artists on their knees to have a show in our gallery.”

“That’s great. I’m happy for you.”

Jenny heard a noise that might have been the sound of grinding teeth, but what had she done to make him angry? Shouldn’t she have some say in this enormous decision to relinquish her art to the world? It was only reasonable.

“Very well,” he said stiffly. Abruptly he bowed and strode out of the studio, heading for the door.

Now Jenny was confused about how matters had been left. Would he still get in touch with her or had she so deeply offended him by not licking his boots that he was done with her?

She dawdled after him, deciding she didn’t care. She noticed that the rush of his departure was slowing as if he were waiting for her to say something. So this was all manipulative behavior, as if he were bargaining for a rug and was pretending to lose interest so that his offer would be accepted. But if his price was bootlicking, the hell with him. He’d come and interrupted her morning, said silly things about her work—she wondered what digitalized mechanical transfer was—and now was being peevish.

At the door he turned and said, “I will come at five o’clock tomorrow for the film.”

Jenny had to admit she was relieved. “I’ll see you then,” she said, smiling in spite of herself. It was almost as big a smile as the one pictured yesterday in the *Mill Valley News.*

14 DEAD MEN

BECK DESCENDED THE FLIGHT OF STEPS to the spot where he'd had the scene with the cyclist who'd shown him his privates and again the image of the man's profusion of body hair flashed in his mind. He was always both attracted to and repulsed by such a coat, having no body hair at all himself—not even eyelashes. He remembered when Jenny's hair grew to her hips, how it had so pleasurably agitated him, and how angry he'd been when she cut it off. She'd had the capacity to disturb him as no one else had— to disturb and defeat him, come to think of it.

And she hadn't changed her exasperating tendencies. She had a way of taking control of a situation simply because she didn't care for things other people cared for: fame, power, success, money. Probably she was still mentally ill.

He got into his rental car, put the key in the ignition, buckled his seatbelt, then felt the muzzle of a gun against his neck. "Yes?" he asked, remaining unperturbed, glancing at the rear-view mirror. Black hair, magnificent mustache, melancholy eyes—the image he saw did not spark a memory.

"Hello, Harry."

The voice was familiar. But his memory was so poor still, so full of holes. His recovery project sometimes seemed hopeless. He despaired at the injury to his previously masterful mind.

"Cousin Harry," the voice said helpfully.

"Horacio," he responded calmly, although his heart stepped up a beat. Of course. Who else? He was the only man in the world who could penetrate his disguises.

"What were you doing at Jenny's?"

"Making her a happy woman. I assure you I left her smiling."

"If you have some scheme to hurt Jenny . . ."

"Aren't you supposed to be dead?"

"Yes. And so are you. Ten years dead."

"You should know, since it was you who killed me." His voice was dry as dust. It almost made Horacio sneeze.

"No, Harry. You shot yourself in the leg and bled to death or, sadly for the world at large, almost to death."

"Why would I shoot myself in the leg, Horacio?"

"Let's go to your place and talk about what you were doing at Jenny's."

"Very well. I think you can safely put the gun away."

Horacio did so, and Harry started the car. Horacio had disguised himself by dyeing his thick gray hair black with a fierce mustache to match. It drooped down at the corners of his mouth, which also tended to droop, what one could see of it. He wore cowboy boots to make himself taller and a straw cowboy hat low on his forehead to obscure his eyes. He wore jeans, a belt with a big silver buckle, and a fitted shirt. He carried a leather satchel over his shoulder, to conceal the Walther. Normally he wouldn't carry a gun, and certainly not a satchel, but when he realized who it was at Jenny's house he seized both. You don't have dealings with Harry without at least one weapon.

The overall effect of his disguise was stunning. He did not look at all like Horacio Huntington, so he was able to amble into Harry's hotel without being recognized, even though it stood in the center of the small town he'd lived in for the past twenty-five years.

It saddened him to be dead to the town and to see it going about its accustomed rounds without him. It gave him a hollow feeling. He felt like a ghost. But he'd been feeling like a ghost long before he rigged his suicide. In fact, today he felt more human than he had in a long time. Life was beginning to interest him again, especially after finding Harry on the scene.

Harry was staying at the new Mill Valley Inn. Number fourteen could have been a room in any nice hotel in any town in America except for the view of California redwood trees and the quixotic furnishings: a blend of New England country and Southwest pastels.

There in Harry's room, the two disguised men, cousins whose fathers were brothers, looked at each other attentively. Horacio did not know what Harry truly looked like since he was always disguised, but somehow, maybe because they looked alike, Horacio always recognized him.

Hairless Harry Huntington was a legendary crime figure wanted by the FBI and Interpol. He was not connected with the Mafia or with any other group. He was his own master and was far out of Horacio's league; Horacio was a one-city jewel thief who stole for fun and adventure, while the range of Harry's activities was staggering, and sinister beyond anyone's ken.

"Not a bad getup," said the king of disguise to Horacio. "The boots are a good touch. The most recognizable thing about a man is his walk. These hobble you."

"They sure do. They're killing me." Horacio pulled them off and dropped them onto the rug. "Damn Mexican boot makers don't allow for a man's toes." He tossed his hat to the top of a standing lamp, making the shot.

"Do you want a drink?" Harry doffed his fedora, laying it on the bureau top.

"No." Horacio watched Harry pour scotch over a single ice cube, thinking how no one in Mill Valley drank scotch. It was wine, beer, *caffe latte*, or sometimes the odd margarita. No one wore coats for that matter. Maybe the reason he always recognized Harry was that he was such a clothes horse. He overdressed no matter what his guise. Why disguise yourself just to stand out like a sore thumb? But it seemed to work for Harry.

"Was it you who left me in those Sonoma hills to die?" Harry asked, shedding the coat as he spoke. Underneath he wore a beautiful gray suit, white shirt, and yellow-figured tie, which he loosened.

"When I took you there, I thought you were already dead. I took your pulse." Horacio seriously wondered if Harry had had a pulse. "You have to understand that it was a hectic time. Arthur was having a heart attack. I'm amazed you survived. How did you get help?"

"I don't know how long I lay there before someone found me. Days. I was in the hospital for a long time and I had amnesia for a while."

"No hard feelings, I hope."

"Don't you remember that I have no feelings?"

"Right," Horacio was relieved. But what about the desire for vengeance? That was more a state of mind than a feeling. Harry might have vengeance on his mind, wanting to exact it. Funny how vengeance is the only thing you exact. Everything else you simply attend to, get around to when you can.

"I remember I had a gun on you at the time . . ." Harry persisted.

"That's what you shot yourself with," Horacio said encouragingly.

"But why would I? It makes no sense. I still haven't recovered my entire memory of the trauma."

Horacio hoped this was true and that it would stay true. "It was a hectic time," he repeated. He certainly wasn't going to assist Harry with his memory recovery. Jenny too had lost her memory for a time. Was he supposed to remember everything for everyone?

"Why would you think I'd die from a shot in the leg? Haven't you ever heard of a tourniquet?"

"All the blood. Thought you'd hit an artery."

"That's why you apply a tourniquet," Harry said furiously.

"At the moment, Arthur was the one I was trying to save."

Harry sipped his scotch. "The doctor told me I had a head wound as well. My skull was badly fractured." Harry's face twitched slightly. Horacio was horrified at this nervous manifestation from Harry, a man of steel. "They were barely able to restore it. It's extremely delicate now, like an eggshell. They should have put in a steel plate, but it was a country hospital."

Horacio paled at the image of an eggshell for a skull. "You must have hit your head on a rock when I dropped you on the ground. I wasn't too careful, thinking you were dead."

"Hmm."

Horacio changed the subject. "Where have you been all this time?"

"Lying low," Harry answered, matching Horacio in his unwillingness to reveal anything. "Living quite differently. Taking advantage of being dead so the police could forget about me. I've become interested in art."

"You were always interested in stealing it."

"I moved to Paris and opened a gallery. I even let myself go around hairless and didn't feel like a freak. You know, people have always found me repulsive."

"Let's just say you scare the shit out of people."

"But I became bored."

"I know the feeling."

"To test my rusty powers I planned an art theft. *Skrieket.* Munch's *Scream.* From the museum in Oslo. It took fifty-five seconds in and out and it's worth fifty-five million dollars. A million dollars a second. I returned it. It was just a test."

Horacio doubted this story. It didn't jibe. Also it was unlike Harry to brag—he must be feeling insecure. Well, who wouldn't, with an eggshell casing around a mind full of holes? "Moving along," Horacio said, "what were you doing at Jenny's?"

Back and forth, the two men pried, each knowing there was no reason to believe the other's answers. Harry poured another drink, sat down in the armchair, enjoying himself. Harry usually did enjoy himself. He was so much smarter than anyone else, and so much more vicious, that he always felt in control.

"I came here to find you, Horacio, to help repossess my memory of the trauma. But you were dead. Then I saw the article in the local paper about Jenny, who I'd totally forgotten. I don't know how much more is still lost but I'm glad I've got her back."

"You sound as if she were important to you. She's not. She was only part of some minor scam of yours years ago."

"That minor scam led to my near-death, which makes it extremely important. You see, I'd always felt myself invincible. This ridiculous scenario of yours does not ring true, this Laurel and Hardy routine of shooting myself in the leg."

Horacio did not like the way Harry harped on the subject. He resisted the desire to squirm. He wished he'd taken a drink, but he couldn't let down his guard.

"Your turn. Tell me why you pretended to commit suicide," Harry asked.

Horacio had been lounging on the bed. Now he got up and wandered about the room in his stockinged feet. One of his socks had a hole in the toe, which Harry looked at with disdain. He studied his cousin's face. Horacio had always been famous for his winning smile, but it looked to Harry like he hadn't smiled for a long time.

"I was serious about the suicide at first. After we lived together for eight years, Jenny left me and I was miserable without her. I couldn't get her back. Life began to turn very gray. I decided to end it all. I sold my house, consolidated my money, arranged to leave it to my kids, avoiding probate, and found I really wanted to leave most of it to Jenny. She needed it. She's off in a dream world half the time. Hopeless. But, it was the money we'd broken up over because she found out I was still a thief and she refused to live off ill-gotten money. The idea of leaving it to her began to amuse me so much I found out I wanted to stick around and see what happened. And of course I wanted to see if she was sorry I was dead."

"Big mistake."

"Yes. It was."

Horacio had been isolated from his friends and family since his pseudo-death, so he found himself relieved to talk about it, even to the unsympathetic Harry. His pain burst out. "Did you see that guy hippity-hopping down the steps this morning, looking like he had the world by the tail? He spent the whole night with Jenny. He must have."

"I saw him, but how did you see him?"

"Never mind. And not only that, she had on her yellow kimono!" His voice cracked. "Maybe I could have handled her being with the guy, but for her to put on the yellow kimono . . . well, you wouldn't understand, but it was a crusher." Horacio clasped his head in his hands.

"What a fool you are." Harry's response was good. It braced Horacio. "I gather she's taking the million," Harry added.

"Did you see that picture of her in the paper?" Horacio asked, looking ill at the memory. "Did that look like a woman who wasn't going to take the million? Or did it look like a woman who not only was suddenly a millionaire but had a new lover to boot—a lover worth wearing the yellow kimono for?"

"Stop wallowing. Emotions have always been your Achilles' heel, Horacio, and turn you into the miserable wretch you are now."

Horacio stopped wallowing. "You still haven't told me what you were doing at Jenny's."

"I'm going to give her a show in Galerie La Vigne. Her paintings are quite marvelous, you know."

"I do know. I've always thought so." Horacio almost found himself warming to Harry. Maybe he was a different man now. Maybe he was human.

But then he reminded himself to look sharp and not believe him. Why would he do something nice for Jenny? He remembered all those years ago that Harry, who was then known as Laveen, had desired Jenny, wanted to possess her. Horacio's skin crawled to think of it.

"Where was Jenny when I shot myself in the leg?" Harry asked.

"Far away," said Horacio. "Far, far away."

"A man who repeats himself," Harry said, "Is usually lying. Didn't Uncle Arthur teach you that?"

15 GRAM

JENNY DRESSED UP FOR GRAM. She put on white linen slacks, a chocolate brown cashmere sweater, pearls. She set the table with linen, flowers, and candles. She brought out the Royal Doulton china that had been her father's and the Tiffany silver. She planned to cook rosemary roasted potatoes, a half leg of lamb covered in Poupon mustard with slivers of garlic stuck into the meat, steamed green beans, and a tomato-and-lettuce salad. Jenny liked to cook.

She hadn't painted as much as she'd hoped, although she'd finished the red chili pepper of the planet Mars. She'd been too excited about the Galerie La Vigne show to concentrate, or to properly lose herself, so she'd given up and gone for a long hike on the mountain, not paying a lot of attention to the birds or flowers, despite her preaching, so deep in thought was she; but the beauty of the mountain nevertheless infused her being as she followed the spider web of narrow trails—the ones the bikers were banned from—which had tire tracks all over them from the recent rains.

She had been tempted to call Sal with the news of the possible Paris show but decided to wait for Beck's final decision before broadcasting it. She would tell Gram, though. And of course Jeff, so he could take the slides. Should she pay him for photographing her paintings? She thought that she should.

She paused in her dinner preparations for a fleeting erotic fantasy about Jeff, and grew aroused. She steeled herself and returned to the task at hand, saving her heightened senses for tomorrow when she could climb into his arms—her pale flesh against his black fur, tongues revolving in each other's mouths, his cloistered cock springing from the density of hair, a heat-seeking missile, no, a heat-and-wet-seeking . . . Well, enough. She had hardly thought about Horacio the entire day, except to think about not thinking about him.

Gram arrived bearing tiger lilies. Her chauffeur followed her up the steps with her overnight bag and a bag of provender including wine, fruit, and some exotic hors d'oeuvres. She wore black slacks with a white silk blouse and a two-toned suede bomber jacket. Her white hair was as short as Jenny's, but in a more stylish cut swept up and away from her face. She wore little makeup and her face was crosshatched with innumerable lines. Her eyes brightened with pleasure at being with her favorite grandchild.

"Well, this place isn't at all the wreck I'd imagined. I expected to find it falling down around your ears. But it's always been so charming, you don't notice the wear and tear. And you look beautiful, darling. No widow's weeds, I see."

Over cocktails and dinner, Jenny told Gram everything. She started to talk about her sadness and loss but quickly segued into her recent, highly-charged affair with Jeff. "I'm just wild about him, Gram. He's so full of spirit, so vigorous. His presence is electric. You never saw such green eyes. They literally flash, like those eyes in bad romance novels."

Gram laughed. "Yes, sex is wonderful. Sometimes we forget."

"But it isn't just the sex. He's smart and funny and talented, too."

"Of course he is," said Gram. "The first week, a new lover is a paragon. It's only later you discover that he's got green contact lenses and his art is derivative. Never mind. Enjoy! I'm glad for you, Jenny."

"But wait until you hear this news. So much has happened since we talked on the phone." Jenny got up to let Abraham outside. From inside, he never scratched or whined but had a way of staring at the door as if willing it to open that always got Jenny's attention. She told Gram about Beck's visit and her possible show at Galerie La Vigne. Then she turned pale. "This is the first time I've spoken the name of the gallery aloud. It sounds like . . ."

"Laveen," said Gram. "The man you might have . . ."

"Killed. The man I did kill—Horacio's cousin Harry. He was using the name Laveen at the time."

"But didn't we decide that he might not have died from your blow with the rock since he'd also shot himself in the leg?"

"You know, Gram, I've taught myself, with Horacio's help, to take full responsibility for that man's death. I struck him in the head with a rock, but I was right to do it since he had a gun and was about to kill us all. If I hadn't thrown the rock, the bullet would have gone into one of us instead of his loathsome leg. It's true that I often find myself hoping I didn't kill him—but, you see, that would mean he was alive, which is a thought too horrible to contemplate." She shivered.

"Good. Then put him out of your mind forever." Gram stood up and tottered for a minute, alarming Jenny, who reached out toward her. Gram, noticing neither totter nor Jenny's gesture, settled square on her feet and spoke commandingly.

"I want you to look to the future. You should accept Horacio's death and get on with your life and your art. Embrace your lover and embrace the idea of this Paris show. It's time for you to get out into the world. Take some chances. Since you left Horacio you have lived so carefully, so reclusively. It isn't healthy. You're definitely ready for a larger arena."

"Do you think so?"

"Absolutely. Go for it."

"Oh, Gram, thank you. You give me courage. And the million? Should I accept it?"

"Good heavens, yes. No question about it. Don't take everything so seriously, Jenny darling. Kick up your heels. You've worked hard at your art. You've loved hard with your Horacio. You've paid your dues. It's time for you to have fun."

They went out to the deck and sat in the old glider. Jenny looked around and listened to the sounds of the night. "The last few days I've been imagining that Horacio is alive, that he's—I don't know. Watching me."

"You're just feeling nervous about the money."

Gram put her arms around her and Jenny put her head on Gram's shoulder, feeling happy, feeling safe.

16 BACKFIRE

HORACIO AND ABRAHAM were on the roof of the trailer, Abraham's chin on Horacio's knee. Through a telescope, Horacio watched Jenny on the glider with Gram. Tonight he would be able to sleep. But what about tomorrow night, and the rest of the nights of his life?

He stood up, dislodging Abraham, and jumped to the ground. Abraham blinked, looked down at the ground and decided to stay where he was.

That afternoon, in his hurry to clean up, change clothes, and get into Harry's Lincoln, Horacio had abandoned his chain saw, belt and ropes by the tree he'd been operating on. Now he coiled the ropes, cleaned and oiled the saw, and put it away in the storage closet of the trailer, all the while thinking of Jenny.

His joke had backfired.

He had spent the months after his "death" in Buserias, a village twenty miles north of Puerto Vallarta, Mexico, where he got a cheap room over a restaurant on the beach and bought himself a blender. Each evening he had made a batch of margaritas to take out onto the balcony or the beach itself, and had watched the soccer games the kids and grownups, mixing it up together, played on the difficult sand, dodging the palm trees on one side and errant roller waves on the other. He had seen the cavorting figures gradually turn to silhouettes before the orange sky then abandon the game in the fading light, dematerializing down the beach.

He would dematerialize down there too, into one of the rickety restaurants where he'd dine on fish and listen to the local mariachis, four aging men in cowboy hats, worn clothes, and handsome boots, whose battered bass, guitars, and accordion stirringly told the tunes while they raised their voices in close harmony against the pounding of the waves, the bass player twirling his venerable instrument at significant passages.

The aimless days had flowed by. He would swim three or four times a day, and walk mile after mile, especially at night when the breakers cracked like a God-sized whip and the moonlight tipped the palm fronds with silver. Sometimes he would throw himself into the *fútbol* fray, although his body, grown arthritic from a lifetime of injuries, always tried to discourage the idea. He had grown his hair and mustache, talked only Spanish, imagined himself content.

Horacio poured himself a cup of coffee and sat down at the cramped table. He felt the trailer shake as Abraham stood up on the roof, then jumped to the ground. Presently he climbed in the open door and settled down on the floor.

"I should have stayed in Mexico, Abraham." Over the last few days, Horacio had broken his rule against talking to dogs.

Abraham had discovered him almost the moment he moved in, dashing across the hill, knocking Horacio off his feet, surprising his master with the intensity of his joy and love. Since then, the dog had been Mr. Cool, as if he was embarrassed by his initial emotional display, but he still spent all the trailer time he could. Horacio didn't feed him so Abraham would be sure to go home periodically to Jenny.

Why didn't I stay in Mexico? Horacio wondered.

All his adult life he'd wondered why, when he was always so happy in Mexico, he never stayed. Maybe it was because he knew the happiness wouldn't last, that his natural restlessness would overcome him. He liked leaving while it was still good between them, so he'd always want to come back. Mexico was the one love relationship of his life that he hadn't managed to wreck. Well, his relationship with Abraham was pretty good, too.

And of course, he had had to get back to play the joke on Jenny, to see what was happening, assuming that Jenny would be grieving for him, pining away, and that she, like Abraham, would be ecstatic to find him alive. That had been his intention, for her to discover in her heart how important he was to her, that he was her life, her love, her only one—as she was his.

So, with a new pair of cowboy boots, a flourishing mustache and hair dyed almost blue-black, he'd returned to Mill Valley, to the property he'd bought next to Jenny's when he had decided not to die after all. He had returned just in time to see the photographer bound up the steps to Jenny's house, and to see the newspaper photo of Jenny blooming from the rich fertilizer of his, Horacio's, ashes, and the subsequent visit of the young man, during which Horacio spent the longest night of his life to be greeted by the yellow dawn and the equally yellow killer kimono. Now he decided to be mad instead of so terribly sad. Okay, his joke had backfired. It hadn't been funny after all. She'd taken the money and a new lover to help her spend it. He knew she'd been sincere about not wanting to live with a thief, not wanting him to be a thief, and he knew that she was genuinely willing to live in near poverty to run her tedious point into the ground. But how could she, or anyone, have resisted a million dollars that had been handed her with the person to whom she was constrained to make the point no longer alive. Poverty can be awfully tiring when you're not sustained by being a purist and an all-around pain in the neck.

He understood all that. He'd grant her the fall from grace, but he wouldn't grant her being so happy about it. After all, he was only two months dead. And here she was—every night a party! With his money! The money she had scorned as too vile and corrupt to touch—as long as he had been part of the package. As he saw it, it was incumbent on him to get his million back. It was a matter of saving face.

He figured he could use Cousin Harry. He had an idea.

Uncle Arthur Huntington, con man extraordinaire, now in swindler's heaven, used to tell Horacio that he was a fine jewel thief, one of the best, but a terrible idea man. He once had said, "You can walk like a cat, hang like a bat, leap like a squirrel, and run like a cheetah"—this was before his arthritis—"and you're the only man I know who can actually smell where diamonds are hidden—just never try anything that takes planning and brains. You're a man of action. In a sudden, desperate situation, your mind takes an intuitive leap and you make the move that is exactly breathtakingly right. But long range, my boy? Don't even think of it. If ever you get an idea that requires making a plan, squash it at birth."

But this was different. This was a good idea. And Harry was part of the plan. He wasn't too proud to ask for the assistance of a genuine mastermind, even one a bit worn around the edges, even one who probably was committed to finding out if Horacio had tried to kill him so he could kill him back.

In a way, the backfired joke had served to fire him up.

17 LOSING CONTROL

THE NEXT DAY SAL CAME TO VISIT, dropping by unexpectedly the way she liked to do. Jenny hoped she'd leave before Jeff showed up to photograph her paintings, and certainly before Beck showed up to collect the film. Jenny still wanted to keep it a secret from Sal until, as they said in Paris, it was *à fait accompli.*

Just as Sal's canvasses were bold, vigorous, and vivid next to Jenny's dowdy paintings of stones, so was Sal a big, beautiful, luscious blonde next to Jenny's slim, non-blonde, muted self. Sal was also a few years younger than Jenny and looked even younger than that.

"Jenny, I just saw a tow truck hauling away the Alfa. Are you getting it fixed?"

"Yes. At last."

"So you've begun to spend?" Sal said. "Good. What else will you do with the million?" She threw herself into the wing chair, all agog to hear. Jenny stood leaning on the mantle beneath her father's portrait.

She didn't think she would tell Sal that Jeff wanted a pool. A pool was going to mean a lot of construction, but when she'd objected, Jeff had said, "We'll have it done when we're in Paris for the show." This had been discussed over lunch today when he'd come by for a brief visit and for, as it turned out, a lot of lively loving in case she'd forgotten, during the night that Gram spent, that sex was currently the most important thing in her life.

"Well," she answered Sal, "The house needs a few repairs. And I intend to be positively wasteful with heat, water, light, and food. I'm counting on you to give me some more ideas."

"Clothes, of course. A whole new wardrobe. You're the only woman left in the world who actually darns her sweaters."

Jenny laughed. "Okay. What else?"

"A total make over! Hair! Skin! Body!"

"New breasts? Forget it."

Just then Jeff came bursting through the door, adrape with cameras, and whipped Jenny into an exaggerated movie embrace so that her back was parallel to the floor. Sal gaped; her jaw dropped so that her lips formed a circle.

"This is Jeff Haymaster," Jenny said, blushing.

"My, my!" said Sal, shaking his hand. "Well, Jenny Hunt, aren't you the sneaky one? How long has this been going on?" Jenny felt embarrassed saying three days. Or was it only two?

"Do you want me to shoot the paintings in the studio?" Jeff asked.

"Yes."

"He's taking pictures of your paintings?" Sal stood up. "What is going on?"

"Well you see—"

"Hasn't Jenny told you about her show in Paris?" asked Jeff.

Sal turned shocked eyes on Jenny as if she'd been betrayed—which, in a way, she had. Here Jenny had a lover and a show, and had begun spending her million dollars, all without her best friend being involved in these enormous changes. Jenny hadn't told her any of this, let alone sought her advice. This was shoddy treatment indeed, said Sal's shocked glance to Jenny's evasive one, better than any words could. Jenny felt like a worm. Jeff, meanwhile, disappeared into the studio.

Before Sal could start up again, Jenny said lamely, "I do not have a show in Paris," just as Beck appeared at the open door.

Sal turned, ready for anything, perhaps wondering whether this man too was going to bend Jenny to the floor.

"Good afternoon," he said, bowing slightly toward each woman. "I have come, as promised, for the film. You understand this is only a formality. I am only going through the motions, as a sop to my partner. I myself have complete faith in your work and would harbor no objections to the show going forward at once."

Sal began to narrow her eyes and to look extremely peeved.

"This is Harry Beck from Galerie La Vigne. Mr. Beck, this is Sal Sorlandio, a famous artist here in California."

"Galerie La Vigne!" Sal almost screamed. "That's one of the top galleries in the world!"

"How kind of you to say so," said Beck.

Now Jenny felt even more guilty. Not only had she gotten a show behind Sal's back and without her help, but it was in the world's best gallery.

"Why don't you have a look at Sal's work while you're in town?" Jenny suggested graciously.

"I'm afraid my time is limited."

"My studio is only a mile away," Sal said quickly. "We could go together from here." Now Jenny saw Sal switch on her charm, go from betrayed friend to belle of the ball, so she excused herself to join Jeff in the studio. She didn't want to stay and watch what could turn into some major bootlicking—but she wished Sal well. Unfortunately, Beck followed close on her heels, and on his heels followed Sal, reeling off the names of galleries where she'd had shows, major collectors who'd purchased her paintings, and museums which had shown or bought her work. Some of these names were outright lies and Jenny was appalled at Sal's desperation. Jenny had always looked up to Sal as a serious and successful artist. Her friend had no need of these absurd exaggerations to impress Beck. Or maybe she did. Maybe she needed to go even further, since Beck didn't seem at all impressed.

Beck blithely turned a deaf ear to Sal's vocal resume, and once in the studio, beamed at Jenny's paintings, and even rubbed his hands together. Jenny felt he was overdoing it.

Sal found Beck's display intolerable and actually began to disparage Jenny's work right in front of her. "Jenny and her little rocks," she began. "She's obsessed with the subject. But she manages to pull it off with some spirit. It only starts to get the tiniest bit boring when you see all the canvasses together."

Jenny couldn't believe what she was hearing. She remembered what Jeff had suggested about her friends' discomfort with the new balance of power in their relationships with her. But Jenny began to suspect that Sal might have been capable of this behavior all along.

"You start to yearn for a flower," Sal was going on, "a blade of grass. Not necessarily a human figure, but something alive—anything to evoke a human response. Some primary color would be nice, too."

Jenny hoped Beck would tell Sal that her rocks were wild unapproachable rocks and perhaps repeat those nice words he'd said about her surface. But maybe she had dreamed it all. Could he really want her paintings hanging in the best gallery in the whole world? Meanwhile Beck and Jeff were getting into an argument about where the best light was for photographing the canvasses—professionals at war. Jenny hoped it wouldn't be resolved by Jeff showing Beck his privates again. Jeff had told her the extraordinary tale at lunch today—Jeff proving, or trying to prove, that he was the dominant male but in the end feeling the loser for not being able to say "fuck you" in the same menacing tone and with the same savoir faire as Beck—although he'd been practicing ever since. Jenny supposed you could only pull the genital-showing stunt one time and that any subsequent display would have a diminishing effect, unless you had somehow gotten bigger in the interval.

Since no one was listening to her, Sal sank into a moody silence. Jenny glanced at her furtively and saw her kick one of the canvasses that was set against the wall. Sal's behavior hurt Jenny but she understood. It wasn't so much that Sal was jealous; it was that she really believed Jenny's work was worthless and Sal couldn't stand this success coming to someone whom she believed deserved it so little, even if it was her own friend. Jenny had heard Sal rage in similar situations when an untalented artist got attention. Her reaction now was mild in comparison.

Jenny suddenly wanted all these people out of her studio. She looked longingly at her constellation, on the easel, covered by a white cloth, and wanted only to be alone, at peace, working. She wondered if she was losing control of her life. It felt like it, but maybe it wasn't a bad thing. Gram had said she'd been too controlled, too careful, too safe, and urged her to kick up her heels. Was this kicking up her heels? Was it fun? She didn't think so, not like painting and having sex were fun.

However, she couldn't rid herself of the feeling that having sex was going to mean putting in a swimming pool—and that would only be the beginning. Luckily, the feeling was also there that life was short and Jeff was worth it. She looked over at him adoringly. He looked back at her and winked. Sal kicked another canvas. Beck asked Sal to leave and she left. Soon after, Beck and Jeff left but still Jenny couldn't paint. There was too much to think about, too much to feel.

18 DOUBLE PROMISE

Cousin Harry effected his eerie mirthless stretch of the lips. "That was my plan," he said to Horacio after Horacio had outlined his idea for getting back the million.

"You mean you never were going to give her a show? You just wanted to rip her off?" Horacio asked.

"Exactly. When I read in the paper that a foolish woman has just inherited a million dollars, it becomes my duty to take the money away from her. It's ripe for the picking. And when the article mentions that her painting has gone unappreciated and unvalued, then I know exactly how to strike."

The cousins were once again at Harry's hotel room, this time on its balcony overlooking the elegant redwood grove, the towering trees of which were straight as telephone poles, a lumberman's dream, practically crying out to be cut into boards. The swooping branches covered with tiny needles and minuscule cones seemed frivolous next to the enormous stately trunks. What became of all of the pretty branches when the ancient forests went to the sawmill, wondered Horacio, he who as a lifelong builder had abetted the crime. But at least he'd made houses, not toilet paper. He liked to believe that the noble trees lived on in his buildings.

Horacio had come to Harry with his plan to recover the money only to find a plan was already underway. It was the day after Harry had picked up the film of Jenny's work to show his partner who, said Harry, didn't exist. There would be no show. Horacio was appalled. It was one thing for him to justifiably recover his own million but quite another for Harry to bilk poor Jenny and break her heart.

"So there is no Galerie La Vigne?"

"Yes there is."

"But you never intended to show Jenny's paintings."

"Of course not. If I sold ten of Jenny's paintings for ten thousand dollars each, which is the most I could get for an unknown artist, I would get my fifty percent—fifty thousand dollars—and it would mean a certain amount of work and expense. This way I get half a million in a few days."

"A half a million?" asked Horacio.

"Yes. I don't think she'd consider them worth a million and anyhow I have another plan for the other half of the money."

"But why not do it my way," insisted Horacio. "Tell her the paintings have fallen into someone else's hands and that person wants the half a million dollars or he'll destroy her life's work. Then, when she's paid the money and gotten the paintings back, you can still show them in your gallery and she won't have to handle the enormous disappointment."

"I want her to be disappointed. You seem to forget who you're dealing with here. I'm not a nice person."

"But what has Jenny ever done to you?"

"Tried to kill me."

Horacio was shocked and frightened. Had Harry remembered? Or was he guessing? "Jenny did not try to kill you," Horacio said levelly. "You shot yourself in the leg. I hauled you away and left you in the hills, thinking," he added hastily, "you were dead. God almighty, how many times do we have to go over this?"

"The more I look at her paintings, the more I seem to remember that she was mentally unstable and given to throwing rocks at whatever troubled her. A man pointing a gun at her and her friends would be troubling."

"Wrong. Jenny collected rocks because it made her feel secure to have them by her side. It's true she was afraid she might throw one and hurt somebody, but she never did. She wasn't even painting rocks that time in Sonoma. She was painting roses, for Christ's sake. She was completely well."

"Why did I shoot myself in the leg?" Harry asked angrily. Horacio couldn't help but reflect that Harry was much more emotional than he used to be. "You can't seem to answer that simple question," Harry said. "Well, I can. It was because Jenny threw a rock at me and ruined my aim."

"Arthur was having a heart attack," Horacio said again as if that explained everything. The line had become a mantra.

Once again he had refused a drink to be on the safe side but now he went to the small refrigerator and took out a bottle of Pacifico. The cold beer slipped down his throat, balm to his inflamed mind and nice on his throat, too. The second one was even nicer.

The beer would make Harry's presence more bearable. There was no one he could talk to except Harry. He missed talking to Jenny, who was so responsive that she made everyone else seem like an emotional invalid—especially Harry.

"Do me a favor," he asked Harry, returning to the balcony, sitting down and propping his booted feet on the railing. "Do it my way. Then it leaves open the possibility of a show for Jenny's work. In the meantime, I can prove to you Jenny is innocent. Although," Horacio couldn't help saying in her defense, "if a person throws a rock at a man holding a gun on her, you can hardly call that a premeditated act. It's thinking and acting fast, doing what you have to do in a desperate moment."

"Nor is holding a gun necessarily a premeditated murder. I wasn't planning a murder at all. I was only holding the gun to . . . to . . . I can't remember." He flushed darkly. "Tell me what happened on that day, Horacio," he asked in what for him was a plaintive voice. "As long as I have these holes in my memory I feel like half a man. It's intolerable."

"I'll tell you if you'll carry out the plan my way. I'll tell you everything when the money's in our hands. Huntington word of honor. Double promise."

“Only the Huntingtons would have to double promise.”

“Arthur once made me triple promise,” Horacio laughed. “But he came through. The Huntingtons always come through. So what do you say?”

“We’ll do it your way.”

“Great! Now tell me something. You probably know as much about art as any man in the world. Is Jenny any good?”

Harry smiled thinly and said, “I’ll tell you afterward. Double promise.”

Now they each had something they wanted to know from the other.

19 CAT BURGLAR

Mill Valley, surrounded by mountain and hills, had steps made of old railroad ties cut into its slopes, so the walker or hiker could go directly from point A to point B without having to take a circuitous road. This way Horacio could get back up to his trailer from town quickly without Harry being able to follow him by car. It was essential that Harry not know where his hidey-hole was.

Where the steps ended he was able to go behind a nearby house and pick up an overland trail that took him to his hillside lot. It was night when he got back to the trailer, which was similar to one he had used at construction sites, only a newer model. The other, seventeen years old, would have been recognized by Jenny. It was badly deteriorated anyway so he'd been glad to replace it. The new white Fleetwood was nineteen feet long with a double bed, galley, bath, and a table with upholstered benches at either side. It was a far cry from his twenty-room house but it served its purpose. He had set it under a spreading Madrone whose smooth orange branches encircled it in a motherly embrace. Twenty miles to the south he could see the lights of San Francisco. To the north, the mountain presided.

Six days ago, as soon as he had gotten back from Mexico, he had bought the trailer and had it delivered to the spot. Over the next couple of days he'd had the electric company set up a temporary pole, and the water company put in a meter to which he had attached a rubber hose. He had dug a hole and filled it with gravel for the sink and shower runoff. He was too far from the sewer line, so he had a chemical toilet delivered, which would be serviced once a week. The trailer had two propane tanks for the stove, but he kept his cooking to a minimum since he didn't have a car to get the tanks refilled.

Once inside, he put a big iron pan over a flame and emptied his backpack of the groceries he'd bought in town. He fried up a steak, mushrooms, onions, and potatoes in the pan. The trailer jiggled to his short steps from galley to table. After eating, he lay on the bed and read a book about Vietnam. It fascinated him to read about a piece of history he'd participated in. Jenny used to say he was looking for an answer to why men marched off to kill and die, time after time, century after century, but no, he just wanted to get a handle on Vietnam, his war, his history. He didn't believe in any larger truths.

After an hour, he put the book aside, tidied up the trailer, dressed in black, changing his boots for running shoes. He went out into the night, creeping over to Jenny's house to see what he could see. If nothing else it was a way to keep up his cat-burglary practice.

Climbing branch by branch, he eased up a California live oak next to her airy ramshackle abode, and from there leapt to the roof, landing noiselessly. He peered through the skylights but couldn't see any sign of her. He thought sourly that Jenny must be deliberately keeping away from the skylights, walking from room to room along the walls.

Then he saw Jeff. Why would Jeff be here and not Jenny? Surely he hadn't moved in. Not so soon. That would be a nightmare. Oh, God, don't let him have moved the hell in!

Jeff was lying on the couch watching television, quite the lord of the manor. Jenny had never had a TV. Horacio tried to see if she'd gotten a VCR as well. Wait a minute, he thought. If Jenny's not there, what's to prevent me from going ahead and robbing the house?

Jeff was there.

That's right, Horacio said to himself with a smile. Dear me. He might discover me in the act of taking Jenny's jewels. There might be a terrible fight. I might have to beat the shit out of him.

Horacio felt a surge of adrenaline course through his body, making him exultant. This was an excellent plan.

"No it isn't!" he imagined Uncle Arthur suddenly calling from the grave. "It's not a plan at all, Horacio, not even an intuitive leap. You're acting like a jackass. Go back to the trailer."

He knew Arthur was right, but the flow of adrenaline was irresistible. He hadn't done anything daring in months.

He remembered Jenny's asinine theory about his thieving just being a hand and foot habit so, just to be fair, he tried it out. He took off his gloves and bit his hands. He viciously kicked one foot, then the other. It was no help. He was still raring to go inside and beat up her new boyfriend. He couldn't wait. Action!

He descended the tree and silently circled the house. He'd persuaded Jenny to install outside lights and she had, but as usual the bulbs needed changing, so the house was dark except for one glimmering living room lamp and the colored light from the TV. He looked through all the windows to be certain Jenny wasn't lurking in some corner. He seemed to remember today was the weekly Life Class in Sausalito, which consisted of drawing nudes, although she'd never portrayed a clothed person in her paintings, let alone a naked one. It kept her hand in, she'd said.

No Jenny to be seen.

It was easy as pie to step into her bedroom window, which opened out and was already ajar. He had only to reach in and crank the handle.

Jenny had some nice family jewels, and some he'd bought for her, too. It seemed a shame to take them but he could always return them later. He pocketed a single strand of pearls, a bracelet with a big brown diamond as centerpiece, and a sapphire ring. He spied the silk kimono hanging from her bedpost and determined to take that too. He rolled it lengthwise and tied it around his waist.

Then he purposely knocked her small bedside clock to the floor and he waited. Abraham trotted into the room, saw Horacio, nodded, and sort of lifted an eyebrow. The dog never made a fuss about seeing his master, no matter how unusual the situation. It was all one to him. His master was not like other men. Nor was Abraham like other dogs.

Horacio heard no other sounds above the basketball game on the TV. He bumped into the table, listened again, finally hearing footsteps. Horacio made for the window as if trying to flee, hoping the guy would have balls enough to come after him and not turn tail and run the other way. Horacio knew the man physically had balls, since Harry had recounted the quirky display the other day on the road.

Jeff came after him. Horacio had one leg up on the sill when Jeff tackled him, pulling Horacio back into the room. To Horacio's joy, they began slugging it out. The only trouble was, the guy could fight. Horacio was sustaining some damage. He'd been goofing off the last few months and wasn't in tiptop shape. Also he was spotting the guy about fifteen years. All the huffing and puffing, grunting and groaning, was coming from his side of the ring. Abraham watched, with a dog's smile, his tail waving. He liked the excitement. Horacio hoped he wouldn't enter the fray, take his side, and give away his identity. At the same time he was disappointed Abraham wasn't jumping in to help him for old times sake. He didn't want anything radical from the old dog, certainly nothing like leaping at the guy's throat, but he might at least worry the man's ankle a little. Maybe Abraham simply had total confidence in his master as the mightier force and would only intervene when his labored huffing and puffing turned to outright calls for help.

A chair came apart as if it had exploded from within. A bedside table crashed and splintered. The two men reeled around the room. The guy was so damned sturdy, Horacio couldn't topple him. His cyclist's legs seemed to root into the rug.

Then Horacio got him up against the bureau and felt he finally had the edge. Now for the quick finish. But it was Horacio himself who went down. The room tilted. He heard Jenny's voice from the living room. "Jeff?"

The sound mobilized him. He had to get out of here fast. Horacio hooked the guy's ankle with his leg, bringing him down. Then, rolling onto his knees, he grabbed his rival's head in both hands. Their eyes locked. Horacio gave the head a good thump against the floor. The glaring green eyes disappeared under lids that fell like shutters as his body went limp.

"Jeff, what's going on?" Jenny was at the bedroom door. In a second she'd reach for the light. Horacio staggered up, tripping on the kimono, which had come loose from his waist and now entangled his ankles. He went sprawling. Jenny screamed and turned on the light. Horacio was back on his feet and diving head first out the window. He somersaulted, regained his feet and took off down into the arroyo in the opposite direction of his trailer.

Somehow he'd grabbed the kimono just before he made his window-dive, and now it fluttered out behind him as he ran, a golden banner rippling in the wind created by the speed of his passage, as his sure feet picked a path through the chaparral. Dressed in black, he was no longer visible so, to Jenny's wondering eyes, the fluttering robe seemed to fly by itself over the bushes beneath the resplendent stars.

"Stop, thief!" she cried, almost to herself.

20 KILLJOY

THE NEXT DAY, Sal came to load Jenny's paintings in the back of her Jeep Cherokee and take them to Pack 'n' Ship to send them to Paris. Harry Beck had called with instructions to go ahead—his partner had okayed the show. Sal told Jenny she wanted to do this favor to make up for her bad grace when she'd first heard about the show.

The truth was that Sal was still simmering with envy and resentment. The whole thing was too unjust. It was Sal who had devoted her life to her art, studied with the right masters, gotten her MFA, had her own students. She had married into high society, from which pinnacle she entertained people who would buy her work. She had doggedly networked in New York, Chicago, and Houston, although it was an enormous drain of her time and energy, to try to develop a reputation beyond the west coast. And she was a damn good painter. It was just that the whole art world was rigged.

Now this unbelievable coup of Jenny's. From out of the blue, an international show. All because of a stupid photograph in the local shopping news and the coincidence of Beck being in town and seeing it even though the picture showed hardly anything of her painting and was in black and white. Why would he go to the trouble and seek her out because of that scrap of a photo, and yet not come to see Sal's paintings even though she was a recognized artist? It was absolutely maddening.

And then for Beck to go to Jenny's studio and actually fall in love with her work. Jenny's art was not what was happening, and it wasn't what was going to happen. He wouldn't get two cents for those pictures. You looked at them and thought, who cares? Jenny's art was boring. It wasn't ugly but it had no depth. Sometimes it got you thinking, sure, although it was hard to say why. It took your mind off humdrum matters perhaps. But painting was meant to engage, to reverberate, to make you exclaim Yes! or even No! Jenny's paintings made Sal think "So what? Pour me a drink." They were a yawn. They were like Jenny herself who, although nice and restful compared to Sal's usual social milieu, was sort of a nonperson.

But now, having coffee with Jenny and hearing the exciting tale of the cat burglar, she almost forgot about this major artistic injustice taking place in their small town.

"But what about Abraham? Didn't he do anything?" Sal asked.

"Jeff said he sort of smiled," Jenny said, smiling herself.

Sal laughed.

"I wanted Jeff to go to the hospital but he said he was okay. He insists he did the most damage but the fact is, Jeff was out cold, and the burglar was out the window like an acrobat."

"What did he get away with?"

Jenny told Sal about the jewels but was uncomfortable mentioning the kimono. Of course it was possible the burglar hadn't meant to take the kimono, just grabbed it spasmodically, but what would he want with the thing? She hadn't told Jeff about the kimono either.

"I suppose this is the downside of having a million dollars. People will come to rob me."

"The upside is a handsome young lover to protect you."

Jenny was thoughtful. "Sal, you sound like you think Jeff is my lover because of the inheritance."

"Oh, were you lovers before?" She pretended innocence.

"No, but—"

"It doesn't matter. Like I said, it's the upside. Whatever works." Sal's vicious mood was descending on her again now that the amusing story was over.

"It does matter. Jeff likes me for myself."

"Of course he does. What's not to like? But a million dollars certainly enhances you."

"Why can't you let me enjoy my good luck? First you make me feel rotten about the show. Now you're undermining the happiness I feel about Jeff. Why are you being such a killjoy?"

"Friends should talk straight to each other."

"Should they? I wonder. I guess it depends where the straight talk is coming from—good nature or bad nature."

"I apologized about bad-mouthing your work and kicking the canvasses. I was upset. I acted badly. But look where I was coming from. Imagine an architect who had never done more than put up tar paper shacks getting selected to design the Taj Mahal."

"Never mind that. We've been over all that. We're talking about Jeff now. He came to take my picture. We hit it off. I can tell when a man is genuinely attracted to me. I wasn't born yesterday. Jeff is not some Euro-trash gigolo slime going around living off older women. He's an all-American boy, a dedicated athlete and photographer. He won the Pulitzer Prize!"

"Good for him. My point is that there's nothing wrong with a million dollars making you more attractive—helping to get someone's attention who maybe would otherwise not notice you."

Jenny sighed. "Let's drop the subject and load up the paintings."

"Yes, let's. I have a tight schedule today."

Jenny and Sal carried the canvasses down to the Jeep, making several trips.

Jenny kissed each painting as it went into the back of the Jeep as if, thought Sal, they were little children she was sending off to camp.

"God knows what this will cost," Jenny said as Sal slid into the driver's seat.

"I'll just use my Visa and collect later."

"Thanks, Sal."

Sal drove away.

21 PIGS IN HEAVEN

"SHE'S NOT TAKING THE PAINTINGS to Pack 'n' Ship." Horacio was on a cellular phone in a stolen Chrysler, talking to Harry in the room at the Mill Valley Inn.

"The bitch is eating her heart out about Jenny getting the show at my gallery," Harry replied. "She's probably going to ditch them somewhere."

"What shall we do?"

The plan had been to follow the paintings from Jenny's house to Pack 'n' Ship and steal them after Sal had left them there.

"Keep following her. You'll just have to wait for the right moment to take them."

"Sal could recognize me."

"I doubt it. Not with your idiotic black eye and broken nose."

Harry had interrogated him about his injuries but Horacio refused to explain. He was losing his awe and fear of Harry, who seemed to him less and less like a criminal mastermind and more like a nagging wife. But then would appear Uncle Arthur's ghost, gin and orange juice in hand, saying, "Harry with half a brain is still ten times smarter than the rest of us and, with half a stony heart, is still ten times more heartless. Stay on your toes, my boy."

"I can't take the paintings directly from her," Horacio said to Harry.

"Knock her out, then. Kill her, if you're worried about her seeing you."

Horacio turned on the wipers as rain splattered down. It was a miserable wet spring. He longed to be back in Buserias. He hadn't been warm since he got home. "She's driving around in circles," he told Harry. "She doesn't know where she's going. She doesn't have a plan." Then: "We're heading out to the freeway. Going north." Five minutes later, he said, "This is unbelievable. I am going to kill her. She's taking Jenny's paintings to the dump. Her life work. How low can you get? I have to act fast before she gets to the gate."

Once past the attendant's booth, Sal could drive into the high-tech indoor dump, toss the paintings into the pit, and a bulldozer would sweep them away along with whatever rubble was alongside. Once in the pit they'd be irrecoverable—except as shreds and splinters.

Horacio fumed at the thought. The magnitude of such a crime against someone who considered you a friend—it was unimaginable.

Sal had been driving recklessly. Now she had to slow down on the narrow road to the booth. Horacio blasted the Chrysler into the back of Sal's Jeep. Sal, furiously wrenching the wheel, pulled over to the side of the road parking next to, amazingly, a corral of gigantic pigs. Horacio saw about fifteen pigs the size of hippopotamuses, snorting, snuffling, and oinking to beat the band.

As a builder famous for keeping a sparkling clean site, Horacio had come as often as twice a week to the dump, and he had never before noticed the pigs.

Horacio parked, dropped the phone in his pocket, and leapt from his car and over to the Jeep before she could get out. There wasn't time to tie a kerchief over his face as he'd intended. Sal was struggling with the air bag, which had inflated in the crash, and didn't see him. Horacio liked a good fight but was not a violent person and had never struck a woman. Luckily he no longer perceived Sal as a woman. She was a rat. So he reached through the window, grabbed her by the back of the neck, doubled his fist and rammed it into the side of her head. Trucks piled high with the detritus of life were inching past the scene but Horacio figured all they could see was him standing at the Jeep window. Sal herself was down on the seat and out for the count. Across the road, at the disposal site, a two-story-high machine started up, thunderously grinding and smashing big waste into small. The noise was so loud it was hard to think. Horacio realized he would be observed switching the paintings to the Chrysler. Better to take the Jeep. But what about Sal? He couldn't put her in the Chrysler.

He walked to the passenger side of the Jeep so he'd be hidden from the road as he checked her pulse. She wouldn't be out long. He wanted to toss her silk-clad form into the pig pen, into the oozing bog of mud and strewn garbage where she belonged, but when he went to the fence he saw the pig pen was remarkably tidy—there was plenty of earth, but no garbage and really no mud except for a glorious single wallow in which one of the pig giants presently was submerged up to his nose and ears. Pig heaven. Horacio savored the thought of Sal regaining consciousness in the wallow. On the far side in separate coops, he saw piglets skittering around in a fancy-footed way that was only a dim memory to their ponderous parents.

Horacio jumped at a sudden, unearthly scream. He looked over at Sal but she was still out. A peacock, of all things, had lighted on the fencepost next to him and spread his wondrous tail. This was a place of many marvels. Jenny would love it here. He would have to bring her when—

Then he realized he couldn't leave Sal in the pig pen. How would she explain it when she was found? She might babble the truth. If Jenny discovered Sal had taken her paintings to the dump, it would break Jenny's heart. No, he would have to take the Jeep with Sal in it.

Back in the car, he wrenched the air bag free from the steering column and covered Sal with it swathing her face and body. With his pocket knife, he cut slits in the bag so she could breathe. He U-turned and drove away, abandoning the Chrysler.

The sun glimmered weakly behind a mass of purple clouds. Rain still drizzled. Off to the east a rainbow reached half an arc upward and disappeared, but not before illuminating the earth and sky. Horacio's heart lifted, as it had always done when he saw a rainbow, ever since he was a boy. It was a good sign. It meant Jenny's paintings were safe. She'd be relieved of her irksome burden of the inherited dough, she'd still get her show, and soon weary of the immature Jeff, she'd be ready to fall in Horacio's arms when his existence was at last revealed to her.

Horacio was no longer mad at her or sad about her. He was prepared to be generous. Since he'd beat up the sturdy lover he felt like a conquering hero, like he'd won Jenny back, even though she didn't know he had. He was her chivalric knight, her protector. He'd saved her paintings and he was shielding her from her crummy friend's betrayal. He was even prepared, maybe, to tell her he'd give up thieving—after he'd stolen back his million, that is, which he simply had to do as a matter of pride and which he was sure Jenny would understand. In fact she'd be glad. It would exonerate her from having fallen so low as to accept the tainted million to begin with. Horacio smiled despite the discomfort of having to rearrange his damaged face to do so.

The best place to leave Sal was at her own house. Ten minutes later he did so, dropping her in front of the wrought iron gates that fronted her driveway, still wrapped in the air bag like a monster baby in swaddling clothes only with the face swaddled too. Another fifteen minutes found him in Harry's room with the paintings.

"The most efficient thing would have been to leave her at the dump," Harry complained after Horacio had recounted the escapade.

"I was afraid Jenny would find out the horrible thing Sal intended to do with her paintings."

"Why shouldn't she know the depths of her friend's iniquity and be able to proceed accordingly in the future?"

"There are some things it's best never to know."

"It's best to know everything," Harry disagreed. "You need every bit of information you can get if you're going to avoid stepping on the land mines of life."

"Easy for you to say. You've never had a friend disappoint you because you've never had a friend. You've never been betrayed because you've never trusted anyone."

"Don't be tiresome, Horacio. Let's go get rid of the Jeep."

"Right. We'll leave it at the Manzanita parking lot where people get the Airporter and buses to the city. That way it won't be found until it gets ticketed. We'll try to find a handicap parking space so as to up the fine."

"You wore gloves, I hope."

"Yes, I wore gloves," Horacio frowned, and pointed to where he had dropped them on the table.

"I have to ask. You're so unpredictable. It's disconcerting to work with you. But it is bringing back memories. The last time, you, Arthur and I worked together, didn't you shoot off your ear?"

Horacio touched his prosthetic ear and said nothing.

"Maybe your black eye and broken nose are actions along the same line, self mutilation toward some mysterious end that still eludes me."

"You think I punched up my own face?"

"Nothing would surprise me." Harry donned his fedora.

"The ear business was only to make it look like I'd been shot at."

"You could have achieved the same effect with a knife. Earlobes bleed profusely. That way you wouldn't have risked your life and destroyed your ear."

"Now you tell me."

"Let's go."

"What about the ransom call?" asked Horacio.

"We'll place it tomorrow. Banks are closed today."

Horacio wanted to hear Jenny's voice. He wished he could talk to her, to tell her about the pigs and the rainbow and the peacock's tail. He would never be able to tell her that he saved her paintings from oblivion but perhaps, in some corner of her soul, she would know, and it would help toward the reblossoming of her love.

22 ON THE PLAZA

GRAM, JENNY, AND MAE were having lunch at the Book Depot Café in the town square, celebrating Jenny's good news about the show. They sat outside in the sun surveying the activity on the brick plaza: skateboarders, hackysack players, guitarists accompanied by mournful voices, chess players at the stone tables by the small redwood grove, mothers, fathers, and toddlers, a congregation of bizarre teenagers, runners back from the Dipsea trail, bending over the fountain one after the other. The rain showers had blown over and the sun shone warmly down when not covered by billowy clouds rolling by. "To think all this used to be a parking lot and a place for smelly old Greyhound buses to pull up to the depot," Jenny said.

"Were you here then?" Mae asked.

"You bet."

"And I was here before the buses, when the railroad came through," Gram smiled, "taking the passengers from the ferry boat that crossed the bay between San Francisco and Sausalito. That was before the Golden Gate Bridge was built."

"Really!" exclaimed Mae.

"Why sure, the bridge is only fifty-eight years old and I'm eighty-one."

"Are you eighty-one, Gram?" Jenny felt a slight panic. "I thought you were still in your seventies."

Jenny wanted to bodily throw herself in front of Gram to ward off old age, sickness, and death—although certainly nothing threatened Gram here in this benign plaza. At the same time Jenny unaccountably felt an almost paralyzing wave of grief for her lost Horacio. Maybe, she thought, recovering, that will be the last wave.

"I wish you were Mae's age," she told Gram.

"I don't." Gram laughed. "I wouldn't be up to all that living, loving, and learning all over again."

"Yeah," said Mae. "It does get plenty tiring."

They laughed.

A band of brawny cyclists pedaled into the plaza, propping their mountain bikes against the iron fence that surrounded the café. The air crackled with their energy and loud voices as if they were still riding and shouting into the wind. Their bright T-shirts were splattered with mud, which they wore like badges of honor. Some of them were splattered with blood as well. Jeff was among them.

Jenny caught his eye and waved. He walked over to their table and she introduced him to Gram. "And you remember Mae."

Some of the other bikers drifted over and Jeff introduced them. He didn't acknowledge Jenny as his girlfriend, didn't happily proclaim her as the woman he'd just moved in with, but maybe these weren't really close friends. Maybe it wasn't their business. Then she wondered if he wasn't subtly letting them suppose Mae was his girlfriend. She felt pain at the thought then berated herself for thinking it. It was Sal's mean comments that were making her sensitive. Most men were not affectionate in public, although Horacio used to hold her hand as they walked along. That had been nice.

Except for the time Jeff had biked her down the hill, this was Jenny's first time in public with him. Could he be ashamed to be with an older woman? Did she really look that much older? She wore baggy shorts and a denim shirt, sleeves rolled up, open at the neck. Horacio used to say her legs were sensational and she knew her skin was smooth and fair—not a freckle, mole, or blemish. She could feel her hair shining in the sun. She knew she was no one to be ashamed of and so smiled happily at Jeff. He smiled back.

Then she followed his eyes to Mae, glowing with a youthful beauty that the shiniest hair, the most flawless skin could not compete with. Jenny felt no envy, though—only pride in Mae as any mother would in a beautiful spirited daughter.

"I'll leave you ladies to your lunch," Jeff said. "See you later, Jenny."

There. He'd said see you later to her. It was not a general see you later, it was specific.

"Very nice," said Gram approvingly, watching Jeff move away, striding awkwardly in his bicycle cleats.

"Mmm-hm," said Mae. "World-class butt for a white man."

Just then another cyclist arrived in the plaza, helmetless, blond hair streaming, riding a road bike rather than a mountain bike. Sal scanned the tables and pedaled over to Jenny. "Thank God I found you," she said, jumping off the bike, "A terrible thing has happened." She was in the same outfit as in the morning: linen pants and silk shirt, now wrinkled and blotched. Jenny had never seen Sal disheveled, let alone dirty, as now. "Jenny, your paintings have been stolen," Sal exclaimed in dismay.

"Jeff!" Jenny called to his receding figure. "Wait! Come back. Something's happened!"

Jeff returned to the table. "Sal says my paintings have been stolen," Jenny told him.

Jeff looked at Sal skeptically. It hadn't yet occurred to Jenny to look at her that way, yet Mae had the same expression as Jeff. So did Gram.

"This car rammed into my Jeep from behind. I was struggling with the air bag when someone hit me. When I came to, I was lying at the side of the road wrapped in the air bag."

"My God!" said Jenny.

"My head was wrapped up too. I was scared to death until I finally struggled free. Waking up in that white cocoon was terrifying—at least to one who is not a caterpillar trying to become a moth."

"And the paintings?" asked Gram dryly.

"Don't I get a drop of sympathy for my ordeal?"

"It was a terrible ordeal," agreed Mae in a flat voice.

"But it was!" exclaimed Jenny with feeling. "Poor Sal. I'm so sorry."

"What about the paintings?" Jeff persisted.

"They're gone. My Jeep too. My brand new Jeep Cherokee!"

"And the other car?" he asked. "The car that hit you?"

"Was gone too. So there must have been two men."

"Where did this all happen?" asked Jenny.

"Good Lord! Do I have to endure this interrogation? Can't I sit down with a glass of wine and be treated as a civilized person, if not as a friend?"

"Oh, Sal, of course, forgive me." Jenny scrambled for a chair, Jeff bringing another for himself. Gram passed her glass of wine to Sal.

Sal ran a hand through her tangled hair. "It was in front of my driveway. I'd gone home to get something I'd forgotten—before going on to Pack 'n' Ship."

"What?" asked Jeff.

"What what?" asked Sal.

"What did you forget?"

Again Sal flared up. "I will not be treated like this. I have been robbed and beaten. I was doing a favor for Jenny and my Jeep has been wrecked and stolen. Jenny's car was too small to take the paintings and she had this luncheon engagement. I was helping her out, not conspiring against her with a ring of international art thieves!"

"But who even knew you were taking the paintings to Pack 'n' Ship?" Jenny wondered. "How many people did you tell?"

"No one. What's to tell? We're not talking Picassos here, God knows. We are not talking Monets."

"So only we knew. And Beck."

"And since Beck is a stranger in town, we can assume he didn't tell anyone."

"I was on a twenty mile ride," Jeff said. "You three were here. Have you reported your car stolen?" he asked Sal.

"Of course I have." Sal glared at him.

"I think we'd better talk to Beck. Let's go over to the Mill Valley Inn. It's only half a block away."

"It's possible he's already left for Paris," Jenny said, standing up and taking her shoulder bag from the back of the chair. The others also stood and gathered their things.

Sal drained Gram's wine and Jenny's too, looking around for more. "Yes, he said his time was limited, too limited to look at my paintings, the shithead."

They crossed the street, Sal and Jeff walking their bikes. "But why would anyone steal my paintings? Sal's right—we're not talking Monets. They're virtually worthless."

"Are they insured?" Gram asked.

"No."

"You should probably expect a ransom call," Gram said.

"Really, do you think so?"

"Well," said Sal, "I hardly think some rich sheik set those thieves upon us to expand his priceless collection. It must be a scheme for ransom—and you're the only one the paintings are worth anything to."

"Maybe Jenny's work isn't that well known yet," said Mae loyally. "But it's about to be."

The desk clerk at the Mill Valley Inn told them Beck was in. They traipsed up to the third floor but there was no answer to their knock.

Horacio was in the room with Harry. Harry told him to hide in the closet, but there was no closet, only an armoire, and Horacio refused to hide in what he called the cupboard. Nor could he fit under the wooden bedstead, with the paintings, and he certainly wasn't going to drop two stories from the balcony, although that would have been a piece of cake in the old days.

"Just don't answer the door," he said. So Harry didn't.

They were quiet until the group had given up and left.

"Okay, let's go ahead and leave the ransom call on Jenny's message machine," Beck said.

"No, I want to call her when she's home so I can talk to her in person."

"Why?"

"To hear her voice."

"You'll hear it on the outgoing message."

"But—"

"Do as I say. Here, put this stone in your mouth to disguise your voice."

Horacio did as Harry said.

23 RANSOM CALL

JENNY DROVE THE ALFA into the garage and sat waiting for Jeff to arrive with his bike. It was wonderful to have wheels again after a year on foot and, since the repairs, the car was running like a top. Maybe she should get a new paint job to cover the dings and scratches, mottles and fades, marring the aubergine color she'd had it custom painted when new. Even though the Alfa was sixteen years old, it only had fifty thousand miles, Jenny being the stay-at-home that she was. Whereas Jeff's VW van, parked next to the Alfa, was only five years old with one hundred and ten thousand miles.

Jeff came careening in on his bike and dismounted. Jenny got out of the Alfa and they walked up the steps together.

"Why were you so harsh on Sal?" she asked him.

"Because she's sabotaged your show out of envy."

"You didn't believe her story?"

"Not a bit."

"You're wrong, Jeff. Sal would never—I know she's volatile but she's an honest, decent person and she's my best friend. Well, except for Gram and Mae. And Horacio."

"Horacio is dead," he said bluntly, as he seemed to do now whenever she mentioned his name.

"I know," she answered in the obedient way she had come to do.

Abraham waited for them at the top of the long flight of steps. He and Jeff eyed each other while Jenny unlocked the door and walked into the house. Shafts of sunlight fell through the skylights in a welcoming way. Jenny thought how nice it was for them to be walking into the house together. She'd been alone for so long. Now she had Jeff and Abraham. She turned to Jeff and put her arms around his neck. Obligingly he kissed her. Then he held her close and kissed her harder. She felt his cock rise against her. It was pleasing how quickly they responded to each other. She felt her pussy swell and seep. But then he gently pushed her away, saying, "I think you should have the police question Sal."

She removed herself from his arms. "I wouldn't dream of it."

"I tell you she's done something with the paintings." His voice was hard. "It was eating her up about the show. Everyone could see it."

"Can't you see that you're making me feel terrible by saying this? I would rather lose the paintings than do something so vile as to wrongly accuse Sal."

He frowned. "Her story was laughable. Whenever I tried to pin her down she flounced around and acted insulted and didn't answer."

"Oh, that's just how Sal is." Jenny laughed. "Poor woman, wrapped in an air bag, left at the side of the road. We really should have given her more sympathy. She was doing me a favor and look what happened. You could tell by her dirty clothes that it really happened, Jeff. She's always impeccable."

She followed him to the refrigerator as she talked. He opened the door to shelves crammed with food and drink, a panorama of plastic bags full of vegetables of every color. Jeff had shopped. He was sharing her checking account. He took out a beer and a bunch of carrots which he washed at the sink.

Jenny put on the kettle for tea. Now that she could drink wine whenever she wanted, she was enjoying her tea again.

Here we are together in the kitchen, she thought, being domestic. Abraham sat patiently by his dish. She told him it wasn't time yet for his kibble so he went and lay down under the dining room table.

"I don't see why you're not upset," Jeff said.

"Well, I am upset, of course. But at the same time, you see, I'm happy too."

"Why?"

"Because of you. Of us. And, I guess, also because of the money. Everything is so great." She looked for a response. Was everything equally great for him? He seemed to be in a bad mood—he was concerned about the theft, no doubt. And, of course, it wasn't great that he'd been beaten unconscious last night. Maybe he was worried about the trip to Paris being scotched.

"I'm sure the paintings will turn up," she reassured him. Then: "Jeff, I'll bet that burglar last night was really after the paintings. He could have seen me drive away and thought the house was empty. No one knows you've moved in." This was an oblique reference to his bicycling friends. Too oblique.

"The television was on and I was sitting in front of it."

"That's true."

Was he in a bad mood because she wasn't going to turn her friend in to the police to be interrogated? If only they'd kept on hugging and kissing each other and not gotten into all this discussion if this even was a discussion. She moved close to him while she waited for the water to boil but felt that he should make the overture this time.

However, he seemed intent on eating carrots, crunching quietly but forcefully in a machinelike way. She imagined his fine white teeth pulverizing the orange fibers, his fine pink tongue hustling them down his throat. Then she noticed the red light flashing on the answering machine on the kitchen counter.

"Ah ha!" she cried gaily. "The ransom call!" She punched the playback button.

Listening intently, she couldn't help but feel that the voice on the tape was Horacio's. The voice was disguised, of course, but it had Horacio's distinctive tone. Now that she thought of it, his voice could have been a model for disguised voices with its muffled droning tonelessness.

She had to play it back again for the content since she'd only listened to the sound. Jeff was finally standing close to her, but not in a sexy way—in a listening way.

"We want five hundred thousand dollars for the paintings or they will be destroyed. Do not inform the police. Get the money from the bank tomorrow morning and we will call with further instructions."

Jeff laughed. "Five hundred thousand! These guys are dreaming. Who are they, the Three Stooges? This is ridiculous." He laughed again. Then he swept her into his arms. He seemed completely cheered up. "Someone's playing a joke on you, baby." He narrowed his eyes and said, "Let's fuck. The carrots have given me strength. Like Popeye and his spinach."

Jenny wanted to talk about the message, but his tongue was in her mouth now, his hand was under her shirt, rubbing her breast and her hand, as if acting on its own, was inside his silken bicycle shorts caressing his resilient, irrepressible member.

Afterwards, after the sex and a drowsy recovery on the bed, seeing that Jeff was asleep, Jenny quietly got up and put on her robe, the bulky bright one Jeff hated, since the kimono was gone. She crept back to the answering machine to replay the message.

Then there Jeff was behind her again, listening too, as if the last half hour had never happened, except they were both in robes now, his a blue terry-cloth.

"It sounds like Horacio's voice," she said.

"It's a disguised voice."

"Well, that's how his voice normally sounds, disguised."

"Listen to me, Jenny." He turned her away from the machine and spoke firmly. "Horacio is dead."

"I know."

"You have to come to grips with his death. The reason you're imagining him everywhere is because you feel guilty about accepting the million and spending it on yourself and on me."

"Really? But I haven't actually bought much so far except for a lot of carrots and other vegetables. Well, the TV and VCR but I would have bought those anyhow. I would have bought the vegetables too. Did you go ahead and buy that new bike you wanted?"

"I bought two."

"Oh. Well, good for you. That's great." She looked around. "Jeff, I have to tell you that I'm going to pay the five hundred thousand to get back my paintings."

"What?" His eyes widened until there was more white than green. "You're kidding!"

"Come sit down on the couch and I'll explain." They arranged themselves one in each corner. "I know we're not talking Monets here. We won't even get into the question of whether they are good art. What's important to me is that the thirteen paintings constitute my life's work—thirty-eight years. To lose them would be like losing my life, like my life hadn't even been."

"You sold seven of them without a qualm," he reminded her.

"But that was okay because I knew they still existed. With someone who loved them. These men, the Three Stooges," she laughed nervously, "are going to destroy them. And there's the show. I want the show now. I'm ready to see what the critics say and see if anyone wants to buy my paintings besides Horacio."

"You can paint more."

"Of course I can. But I can't paint now what I painted then. Every painting stands for growth, in myself and in my art. They are steps on a ladder and to lose them would be like having the ladder swept out from under me. I'm terrified that it might even seem pointless to me to keep on painting with my foundation gone, and if I can't paint I might as well not exist.

"So they're worth five hundred thousand to me, Jeff. We'll still have half a million left. We can go to Paris and put in the pool and have lots left over. The good thing is that I decided to spread the million over seven different banks until I decided how to invest it, so it won't be a big deal to take a hundred thousand from five of them."

Jeff was thinking gloomily, five hundred K for those rinkydink rocks. He realized this setup wasn't going to work. She was too wrapped up in her art and in her fucking lost Horacio to give him the time of day. Sure she liked him okay and was generous too, but he was nowhere next to her art and her dead lover. He had to be number one in a relationship. Hell, she even put Gram and Mae before him. An old lady, a black kid, and a ghost were her best friends before him. He was just her stud. Granted, that's how and why he'd insinuated himself into her life but now it griped the hell out of him. And she hadn't even listened to him about Sal. Everyone was more important to her than he was. And look, there she was wearing that bathrobe she knew he hated. If that didn't tell the whole tale right there, what did?

Abraham came over to the couch and looked at Jenny blearily. This masterful bleary look was one she often tried to imitate with little success, just as Jeff failed to imitate Beck's menacing admonition. Sometimes, thought Jenny, you needed a whole lifetime experience behind you to be able to look or sound a certain way.

24 ANGER

Jeff's anger with Jenny was not for the reasons he'd given himself—the bathrobe was the least of it. His anger was with himself. Jenny's discipline and her respect for her art and for herself were anathema to him. He had never encountered anyone like her.

He had begun his career as a talented photographer. He'd won a Pulitzer. Maybe it had been luck, like his father had said, just being in the right place at the right time, but Jeff had talent too. However, he had not worked particularly hard at his photography before the prize, and afterwards he rode on the fame for all it was worth and hardly worked at all. Fame and success, of course, were everything. He never would have spent his life as Jenny had, working hard without trying to make a name for himself. Then he became obsessed with cycling and spent less and less time at his job until he lost it, took lesser jobs, and now was nothing more than a hack photographer for a shopping news.

Now for the first time he was seeing someone's genuine devotion to her craft and it made him angry, although he didn't know exactly why.

Racing took discipline. He wasn't top ranked but he was getting there. If he spent the same amount of time and energy on photography as he did on cycling, he could regain his prestige. But work didn't have the same rewarding sensations as bicycling: exhilaration, the camaraderie, a hard body, and the adrenaline rush as he ripped down some banned mountain trail like a terrorist heedless of anything or anyone in his path. Cycling made him feel great—the great feeling wore off pretty quick but could be regained on the next day's ride. It wasn't exactly happiness, which was what Jenny seemed to feel a lot of the time; but it was a feeling worth recovering day after day. Craving the great feeling, satisfying the craving, covered his ongoing anger at himself.

Now he allowed in his anger—didn't deny it, only denied it was at himself, told himself it was at Jenny, and believed it.

Why was she wearing the detestable bathrobe when he'd said how lovely she looked in the kimono and had taken an unbudging position on this blaring fuzzy one at the outset? She must have known it was like waving a red cape at a bull. She was asking for trouble.

He watched her as she fed Abraham. In that robe she looked like somebody's landlady—somebody's old landlady.

She sat back on the couch, reading his mind, which wasn't hard to do. "The thief took my kimono," she said.

Jeff recognized this as one of those moments that made life with Jenny so interesting. A burglar had come in the night and taken, along with the jewels, her kimono.

"I saw it in his hands as he was escaping. Strange, isn't it? Maybe he didn't realize he had it. Or perhaps he thought it was still valuable. It used to be when it was Gram's."

"You saw him running away? What did he look like?"

"I don't know. I just saw the kimono. Maybe he was using it as a diversion, so I'd look at it instead of him, like male birds do with their plumage, or magicians do with scarves."

"I suppose you think the burglar was Horacio," Jeff said bitterly.

"Horacio's dead," she said.

Jeff scowled. He was nursing his anger, getting off on it. What irked him most of all was her disregard for her inheritance. She was willing to deprive him of half her money to get back a bunch of paintings of the same old rocks which she could, in his opinion, easily paint again. Why should the thieves get such an enormous sum? They shouldn't—he should.

"I'll deliver the money for you," he said. "I'll make the exchange."

Jenny's face lit up. "Thank you for being so understanding."

25 IN THE GARAGE

THE NEXT MORNING, Horacio, up in a tall eucalyptus tree, watched Jenny leave for the bank, her short shiny hair ruffling in the breeze of the Alfa. An hour later he watched her return, garage the car, and climb the steps carrying what she called her portmanteau, a strong rattan bag bigger than a briefcase, smaller than a suitcase. It was the bag she used to take on their weekends away, proud she could pack so small.

Now she would sit by the phone and await instructions.

He climbed down the tree, followed a trail hidden from the house to the road, and stepped into the garage, which was tucked into the bottom of the hill at the foot of the steps. He wore blue jeans, a blue work shirt, and the straw cowboy hat. His gun and his cellular phone were tucked into a leather tool belt. Around his neck was a red and white cotton bandanna.

He stepped through the back door and stood in the murky cement-colored light. There was little of the flotsam and jetsam most garages accumulated. There were some garden tools, a few cartons. Jenny was not a hoarder.

During the night, while snooping around, doing the self-prescribed amount of skylight peeping, he'd seen Jeff make a suspicious trip to the garage while Jenny slept, so now he looked to see if there was anything out of place or missing.

The van was locked and the curtains were drawn across the windows. He stepped up on the front bumper and peered through the windshield. He saw two bicycles and a stuffed duffel bag inside. It looked like Jeff had plans.

From his pocket, Horacio took the stone Harry had given him to disguise his voice, put it in his mouth and dialed Jenny's number on the phone, covering the mouthpiece with the bandanna. When she answered, "Yes?" he was so glad to hear her voice he almost cried, "Jenny, it's me! I'm home!"

Instead he droningly told her to go to the telephone booth at the Chevron station across from the Fountain Motel to await further instructions.

"Is it okay if my friend takes the money for me?"

Horacio pondered. "All right. You remain at the house."

Horacio crouched down by the driver's door of the van. Now he tied the bandanna around his face and pulled the hat brim low over his eyes, especially his black one. If Jeff took the Alfa, he was on the up-and-up and Horacio would not be discovered. If he took the van, that was another story: the blowing-town story. Remembering how the guy's legs seemed to root into the rug, Horacio was glad he had a gun and didn't have to fight him. Jeff's legs rooting into the cement would be worse.

Jeff entered the back door of the garage, carrying Jenny's portmanteau, squeezing past the Alfa and unlocking the driver's door of the van.

"Drop the bag." Horacio almost said "portmanteau," which would have given him away, but he caught himself. "Put your hands up. Turn around and face the wall."

Jeff did.

"You're planning to run out on her, aren't you?" Horacio asked, the stone still in his mouth.

"What's it to you?"

"You don't care about the paintings. You don't care about her. You just figured you can get half a mil for free. She wouldn't even report it missing, knowing her. You scumbag. You good-for-nothing bastard. You're not fit to lick her boots."

"I was plenty fit to lick her cunt."

Horacio almost swallowed the stone and his inward gasp also drew the bandanna into his mouth. Between the two, he almost choked. The garage turned black and crowded, seemed suddenly crammed with cartons pressing in on him. Gasping and sputtering he caught his breath and he found himself admiring Jeff for standing up to a man with a gun, not caring what he said.

"Don't tell me you're Horacio!"

Horacio spat the stone onto the cement floor. Jeff started to turn his head at the sound. "Don't move," Horacio warned.

"If you are Horacio, you're the one treating her like dirt. What's this all about? Are you crazy?"

Horacio considered this last question. There could be something to this idea. Was he acting crazy? His behavior made perfect sense to him, but to anyone else it might not. This was pretty much how he'd been all his life. It was nothing new. He was an outlaw.

Was he treating Jenny badly? It seemed to him he was protecting her from her false friends, Sal and Jeff, who Jenny wrongly trusted.

"Take those bikes and bag out of your van. Leave them here. Go to the phone booth and you'll be told where the paintings are. When you come back, if you still want to leave Jenny, tell her like a man. Tell her why. And I suggest you do leave her, because she's going to find out that you don't give a damn about her. She's not a fool."

"She was certainly a fool to ever get involved with you. Maybe I better stick around to make sure you don't crawl back into her life and muck it all up just when she's beginning to be happy. She was a fool, grieving for a jerk like you. You've only tricked her all along. You leave her money just so you can steal it back! Just when her life is starting to improve from the dire poverty you allowed her to live in before."

This was totally unjust! Jenny had left him! She had refused to live on what she perceived to be tainted money and had refused any help from him. He had had to furtively buy her paintings just to keep her going, then he had left her a million dollars with a good heart. He was only stealing it back because she was supposed to have refused it, and because of this thieving bastard standing in front of him who had moved in on her and the money who now dared to accuse him of mucking up Jenny's life when he himself was about to run out on her with half her fortune! Horacio was entitled to steal this money, Jeff was not: that was how Horacio saw it.

Harry would not approve of this twist in the operation. It was not part of the plan that Horacio dictate Jeff's romantic behavior. But Harry would approve of Horacio's guess that Jeff had planned to take off with the money himself instead of delivering it to them.

Horacio decided to lay it on the line. "You do right by Jenny or I'll kill you."

"Go ahead, then, shoot me now, because I'll do what I fucking want."

Horacio considered it, but murder was not in his nature. He had never killed anyone, and he wasn't going to now. But he admired the guy's unflappability, his stone cold cool. He was like a miniature Hairless Harry Huntington with hair. He remembered how he'd shown his pecker to Harry, and bragged about his cunnilingus to Horacio. Was this the new generation, to be so overtly sexual? Never mind. It was he, Horacio, who had the gun.

"Move the bikes out of the van."

Jeff did. Horacio noticed they were new. One was a Steve Potts, a local bike maker whose hand-crafted mountain bikes went for around five thousand dollars. How could Jenny be such a fool as to lavish money on this scum? Jeff had clearly taken advantage of her vulnerability during her time of grief.

"Now get moving," Horacio said. "The money stays with me."

Jeff made a move toward the car but suddenly whirled around, his leg in the air. The gun flew from Horacio's hand. At the same time, Jeff lunged forward and grabbed for the portmanteau. Horacio, surprised and off balance, managed to keep his grasp. The two started a vicious and silent tug of war with the bag, each digging in his heels, trying to pull the other over.

Horacio was determined that the younger man would go down, but suddenly Jeff followed Horacio's pull instead of resisting it and Horacio lost his footing. Jeff yanked the bag away and swung it at Horacio's head. Horacio ducked. His hat went flying but his head was undamaged and he let the impetus of his feint carry him to the floor where the gun was. In one quick movement he rose to his feet and leveled the Walther at Jeff.

"As I was saying," Horacio said, trying not to pant from his exertions over the bag. He wanted to prove who was the better man, irritated as hell that Jeff wasn't bruised from their fight two nights before. It wasn't right for the winner's eye to be the blackened one. People would get the wrong idea about who the knight errant was around here. Horacio was also peeved that Jeff had disarmed him. He's not that good, Horacio told himself. It was a lucky kick.

But all this was trivial. It occurred to Horacio that maybe the joke on Jenny had gotten out of control, that the man he should be worrying about was not Jeff but Harry. The million was not the main issue here. His and Jenny's lives were.

"As I was saying," he said, more steadily, "the portmanteau stays with me."

26 CONFESSION

JENNY WAS NERVOUS about the exchange of money for her paintings, and it didn't help that Sal came over half an hour after Jeff had left. She preferred to be alone with Abraham. Still, Sal had been involved from the outset and felt she had a proprietorial right to know what was transpiring.

Strangely, Sal was still dressed in the dirty clothes of yesterday. Her makeup was slapdash and her hair hung in snarls and snaggles. Jenny decided not to comment. She herself had dressed nicely to make the withdrawals from the five banks. She wore the (darned) cashmere sweater and linen pants she had worn the night Gram came to dinner.

She sat in the wing chair by the window with Abraham stretched out at her feet and told Sal about the ransom call yesterday and the follow-up one this morning. When she said she was paying five hundred thousand for the return of the paintings, Sal screamed and looked faint. Jenny decided not to repeat the rationale she'd told Jeff. If Sal, a fellow artist, didn't grasp at once the value of her entire life's work, then the hell with it. Instead, she ignored Sal's histrionics, and said, "Jeff left with the money about a half hour ago to make the exchange."

More screams. Sal clasped her brow and reeled around the room. "You trusted Jeff with all that money! What do you know about him? Nothing. Good God in heaven, we should call the police right now! Do you have his van's license number?"

"Of course I don't. I completely trust him."

"Oh, Jenny! You've only known him a week. He's a complete stranger. For all we know he's in on the whole scam. It's the only thing that makes sense." Jenny didn't say that Jeff thought Sal was behind the whole scam and that was what made sense to him. "Or he and Beck could be in it together. They both appeared in your life the same day. Maybe Beck is not Beck and never planned to show your work to begin with."

Jenny wished that Sal would go away, but Sal paced the room, presumably thinking. "I've got an idea. Why don't you call Galerie La Vigne in Paris and ask if Harry Beck is the owner? And ask if they're planning a show by Jenny Hunt."

"That's a good idea. But I don't want to tie up the phone just now. Jeff may try to call."

"You're crazy if you think you'll ever hear from that guy again. Mark my words."

"You are going to have to eat your words," Jenny said grimly. "Until then please shut up about it."

Sal looked startled. Of course, she didn't know Jenny had defended her just as vigorously the night before.

"I'm only warning you for your own good. I'm just trying to look out for you." After a few seconds she asked, "How about if I use my car phone? I'll call Galerie La Vigne for you."

"You found your car?"

"The police found it at Manzanita. In crippled parking, wouldn't you know, so my fine is comparable to my annual property tax. They dusted it for prints. I'm on my way to the body shop this afternoon. So, should I make the call to Paris?"

Jenny did think it was a good idea. "I'll call, if you'll bring me the phone. I should be the one to do it. It's my business."

"You don't trust me, do you? You think I'll try to ruin the show. I hate women like you who, when they get a lover they've known for two days, completely forget their women friends they've known for twelve years. Ever since you've been with Jeff you haven't confided in me about anything. You've kept secrets from me. Now you don't trust me to make a simple call for you that could actually shed some light on this nerve-wracking nightmare that has mostly been my ordeal."

Jenny gave Sal the Bleary Look and felt that under the stress of the moment she'd done a creditable job. She really needed to simultaneously hang out her tongue like Abraham did to achieve the full effect, which was to say: "I have completely run out of patience. We will not discuss this any more. I'm the boss around here and you are an underling."

Sal got the message instantly. "I'm going right now to get the phone," she said.

While Sal was gone, Jenny said to Abraham, "All this fuss is about money, Abraham. It isn't about love, truth, beauty, or art. You're so lucky to be a dog. You have your priorities straight and money isn't one of them. Loyalty, kibble, bitches in heat, shade from the sun, shelter from the cold, chaseable cats, plenty of sleep. Especially loyalty. I'm trying to stay loyal to everyone but it's hard."

Abraham grunted in sympathy.

Sal, breathless from step-climbing and the current excitement—which she considered her ordeal, not Jenny's—returned with the phone. Jenny tracked down Harry Beck's card, returned to her chair and punched in the numbers. A man's voice answered, "Galerie La Vigne."

"Monsieur Harry Beck, *s'il vous plait.*"

"He is in California," the voice replied in English.

This was great news. Jenny was thrilled and relieved. "Are you Mr. Beck's partner?" she asked, warming to the man who had agreed on the show.

"I work for him. I am his associate."

"My name is Jenny Hunt. You have arranged for a show of my paintings."

There was a pause. "This I have not heard about."

"Have you been in touch with Mr. Beck?"

"I talk to him every day."

"Did he send you a roll of film of my work?"

"No, madam." Pause.

"Would he have done so were he planning a show?"

"It is possible he would ask my opinion, but it is his gallery."

"I see. Thank you. Good-bye."

Jenny clicked off the cel phone. She felt—strange, sort of dead. She was suffering a severe loss of confidence. Sal was right. They weren't talking Monets. They weren't talking art at all. She was no good. Before, she hadn't really thought about whether she was good. She had just painted, worked hard, and had been happy. Then Beck had told her she was good, had offered her a show in the best gallery in the world, and she had believed him. She had felt a little suspicious about him at first but then had trusted that he was who he said he was and that the show was truly to be.

And he was Beck—but the show was not to be. So he must be part of the scam. Why a reputable gallery owner would come all the way from Paris to bilk her out of her money she had no idea. But, it didn't matter at this point. Nothing mattered.

"What?" Sal paled seeing Jenny so stricken. "What did he say?"

"You're right. There's no show. His associate's never heard of me." Her voice came out a dry husk.

"Oh, Jenny. I don't want to be right. Not now. Not any more. Jenny," Sal threw herself down on her knees in front of Jenny, "Forgive me. I have been bad. So bad."

"Forget it." Jenny didn't want to talk to Sal about her badness. She wanted to suffer her disappointment in silence, try to come to grips with it.

"No. Let me tell you." Sal looked beseechingly at her. "I was so jealous. I couldn't stand it."

"So you said some regrettable things. I understand. Let it go."

"It isn't what I said. It's what I did. You see, I wasn't ever going to take your paintings to Pack 'n' Ship."

"Please, Sal—I want to be alone now." Wispy voice.

"No. I have to confess or I won't be able to live with myself. Because here you are suffering this huge disappointment. I should have rejoiced at your good news. You completely deserved it. But all I could think of was how to ruin it for you. After we put the paintings in the Jeep, I just drove around with them. I didn't know where I was going but I knew it wasn't to Pack 'n' Ship. Those paintings were never going to see Paris, was the idea that was fixed in my mind. Then I realized where I was going. To the dump. I intended to throw your paintings in the dump. That was my decision."

"No!"

"Yes. That's where I was headed when the thief crashed into me. He really did leave me wrapped in the bag at my house, but the rest of it happened at the dump. He stopped me in the nick of time."

"You could never have destroyed my paintings, Sal." Jenny's voice trembled, was barely a whisper.

"I pray that I wouldn't have, that I'm not so unutterably loathsome, but we'll never know, will we? I was mighty close. I was almost to the entrance. All out of envy and malice. I'm a horrible person." Sal started to cry, to actually lay her head at Jenny's feet and sob, but Jenny could not reach down to comfort her. She was too hurt. She could not tell Sal that she was not a horrible person—it would be a lie. Sal's behavior was beyond Jenny's comprehension. And it was not that Sal had had anything to gain by her action—it was that Jenny had had everything to lose.

"Tell me you forgive me, Jenny."

Jenny was a great believer in forgiveness. You had only to apologize and Jenny would forgive you as a matter of course. But now her voice had deserted her, and so had her powers of forgiveness.

"I'll do anything to make it up to you. I'll show slides of your work to all the gallery owners I know. I'll give you a show myself if I have to."

Sal's prattling was intolerable but Jenny couldn't find her voice to say so. She stood up and, still unable to speak, waved Sal away, like a referee calling an incomplete and then an out of bounds.

"What?" Sal unsteadily rose to her feet from her crouch. "You want me to go?"

Abraham stood up, moved in front of Sal and growled. The hair on his neck bristled, standing out like a lion's mane. His legs were rigid as sticks. His teeth gleamed as he savagely growled again. Sal was frightened. Old Abraham standing by Jenny in her hour of need. He had found Jenny's voice.

27 IN THE TRAILER

After Jeff drove off in the van, Horacio tore a bag from a green roll on the garage shelf and emptied the portmanteau of the money, tipping it all into the bag, then knotting it at the top. Dressed in work clothes, he would be less noticeable carrying a plastic bag than an elegant rattan number.

He slipped out the back door and stood blinking in the sun. The day had turned warm and bright. The wind had died. A flock of quarreling birds had taken over the spiky quince bush that grew against the garage intertwined with the rampantly growing blackberry. Horacio made his way along the road then up the trail and over to his building site. He figured he looked like one of the many Mexican workers that were proliferating in the county. Under the dappled light of the big madrone, he opened the trailer door and stepped inside. Something crashed against the back of his head and two interiors turned black—the inside of the trailer and the inside of his mind.

When he came to, he was lying face down on his bed, his hands tied behind his back, his ankles tied together, a rope connecting them. Slowly, he turned over and managed to get into a semi-sitting position, slumped against the wall. Moving even slightly was murder on his head. He looked down at the bed to see if he'd left any skull parts there. He felt like there were pieces missing. He saw splashes of blood on the striped comforter but no cranium splinters or brains. Then he looked up and over.

A stranger was sitting at the table. He was dressed not unlike Horacio in blue jeans and a blue work shirt, a baseball cap on his head. His body was neither fat nor thin and he did not look particularly strong. His eyes were a penetrating icy blue that made Horacio feel the man didn't need physical strength in order to get along—and didn't need to be liked either. Not a people pleaser. Even if their circumstances were reversed, and Blue Eyes was the one who was hog-tied, Horacio didn't think he would like him.

The rest of the trailer was unchanged, except the light was dimmer, as if the sun was behind a cloud. Maybe his eyes were going or gone. He looked to see if his eyeballs were on the bed. The bag of money was at the door where he must have dropped it when he was slugged. Why hadn't the guy taken the money and run? His belt with phone and gun had been removed and tossed on the floor by the bag.

"Lost your way?" Horacio asked.

"It's me, Horacio."

Horacio couldn't connect. "Me, who?"

"I must have hit you too hard."

"Harry?"

"I guess this is the first time you've seen me undisguised—*au naturel*."

"What's this all about? Did you think I'd take the money? You can have it. I don't care anymore."

"I don't care anymore either."

"Jeff cares. He was running out on Jenny when I took it from him in her garage. But, why don't you care?"

"I only want information. What you have to understand about me, Horacio, is that my most important possession is my ego. I have to be the best. Ten years ago, someone bested me. That left my ego with a big injury. It changed me."

"I've noticed."

"Have you?"

"Yes, you're not the man you were. You are more"—Horacio decided not to say *insecure*—"human, I suppose. Nothing wrong with that."

"Yes, there is. Look at you: you're not worth a damn in this business. You let your feelings get in the way all the time. Arthur was right about you. I won't even ask what passed between you and Jeff when you got the money."

Horacio changed the subject. "How did you find out about the trailer?"

"I paid a kid to tail you one day. Someone you wouldn't notice."

"I never figured you for hoofing it anywhere so I felt safe taking the trails."

"You said you would tell me everything about my murder when the money was in our hands. Now's your chance. I'm sure Jenny did it. I remember the rock."

"No, Harry. I threw the rock."

Harry sat so still, he might have been the one tied up. Horacio wished he were. Then Harry stood up and glared down at Horacio, almost shouting at him, "You've told me ad nauseam you were taking care of Arthur at the time, because of his heart attack." He slapped Horacio's face. "Well?"

Horacio's mind scrambled forwards. His ears were ringing. "That was after I threw the rock. I had asked him to help me dump your body in the hills and that's when his heart gave out on him. I helped him to his room. His dying words were for me to look after Jenny. Little did he know the burden he was laying on me—you have no idea how hard she is to look after. Now will you untie me?"

"Where was Jenny?"

"She'd fainted."

"I think I'll have to hear Jenny's side. I think it's time she found out you're alive."

"You've got to believe me. I double promised. And what about your promise? You were going to tell me how good an artist Jenny is."

"I said I would when it was over. I meant all over."

"How will we know when it's over?"

"I'll know," Harry promised, but Horacio had the feeling it wouldn't be over for Harry until Horacio and Jenny were dead.

"Tell me now."

"Very well," began Harry. "Jenny paints because she wants to, because she is compelled. She doesn't paint to sell, or to get into museums, or even to decorate her house. The only picture she has hung is one of her father in his flying gear—painted before she was born. She paints from life, but also from imagination. And her technique is superb. She studied other artists but isn't derivative. There is freshness and originality in her work."

"So, cut to the chase—is she good?"

"It doesn't matter, Horacio."

"I want to know."

"A good artist is one who breaks new ground."

"Does Jenny?"

Harry got up, put a black leather jacket over his denim shirt and took off his cap, revealing his hairless head. He put on dark glasses, darker than the tinted ones he'd worn before, and a beret. "I'm leaving you for a little while. I don't think I need to gag you. Somehow I can't imagine you yelling. It's not your style and besides no one could hear you." Harry left, taking the bag of money he didn't care about.

Horacio didn't have a yell in him—that was part of his voice trouble, just as Abraham didn't have a bark. Horacio knew that even bound, he could probably get out of the trailer and roll and slide down the hill to the road. But just as it wasn't his style to yell, neither was it his style to lie hog-tied at the side of the road, his face in the dirt, until someone came to help him. What if Jenny found him that way? It would be humiliating. He would not at all appear to be her knight errant, her chivalric protector. He would appear to be a pitiable stupid jackass. Better to await developments. Better to sleep. Besides, Abraham would come along soon and chew through the ropes.

Briefly Horacio thought about worming his way over to the tool belt to see if the phone and gun were still there but Harry was not a fool. Even if they were there and he could punch out a phone number with his nose, who would a dead man call? If he could pull the trigger with his nose, who would he shoot at?

Horacio didn't want Jenny to know he was alive. If he could roll out of the trailer and slide down the hill all the way to Buserias, that would be good. But he had to stick around and make sure Jenny survived Harry and he had to stick around because he was tied up and his head was killing him. Horacio could not think straight. He slept.

When he woke up his head felt better but his arms were cramped. A sound at the door had awakened him. Good dog!

But it wasn't Abraham—it was Sal.

"Oh, I'm terribly sorry," she said. "I thought I saw someone I know come this way a while ago—my goodness! Are you tied up? Can I help you?" Horacio nodded vigorously whereupon Sal asked, "But why are you tied up?"

Horacio decided to pass himself off as a Mexican. "*No estoy ligado por ninguna razón,*" he told her. "*Por favor, desligame.*"

Sal looked bewildered.

"I myself was in a similar situation yesterday so I know it's no fun," Sal confided. "I wasn't exactly tied up—wrapped up, which in a way is worse. I couldn't see anything. You at least have a nice bed to repose on whereas I was left at the side of the road like a sack of garbage."

Garbage reminded Sal of her confession of the dump and of Jenny's horrified response. Which was why she was looking for Harry Beck now, to do what she could to resurrect Jenny's show at Galerie La Vigne, even if it meant paying him to do so.

Sal tried to remember the Spanish to instruct her cleaning lady. "*Conoce usted Señor Beck?* He promised my friend Jenny a show and it turned out to be utter hogwash."

Hogwash reminded Sal of the dump. She had a terrible feeling that everything she did and said from now on would remind her of the dump and of having sunk so low—unless she could make things right.

"*Por favor.*" Horacio turned his back and displayed his bonds. He was upset to learn there was to be no show but wondered why Sal was upset about it. She had done everything in her power to see to it that Jenny's paintings never got to the show or got anywhere.

"I don't think I should untie you especially if you're an amigo of that rat Beck." Rats, too, reminded her of the dump. "What an adorable trailer. Do you live here while you're clearing the land? You could do a lot worse, prices being what they are here in Marin. I love this miniature kitchen! And look," she said, opening the bathroom door, "you even have a whole bathroom."

Horacio was furious at her snooping. The nerve of her, walking into a man's home and poking her nose around which he knew she would not do if he were a white man, even a tied-up white man.

"Not much closet space, though," Sal chirped. "I'd need much more closet space." As if a poor Mexican gave a shit how much closet space she needed. "That's funny. Haven't I seen that kimono before?"

"*Por favor, Señorita.*" Horacio said loudly. He showed her his bonds again, tugging at them and wriggling so as to drive the point home to the stupid bitch.

Sal ignored him and sat down at the table. "I did a terrible thing. You wouldn't understand even if you could speak English but, you see, I have this friend who paints and I took all her pictures to send to Paris for a show but instead, I took them to the dump. I don't know what got into me. I was in the grip of an envy so fierce it unhinged me. It's frightening. I thought I was a decent person. But I'm not.

"The paintings were saved—never mind how—but it turns out there is no Paris show. Jenny was crushed. I confessed to her what I had done. She threw me out. Well, her dog threw me out—sweet old Abraham turned into a snarling monster like—who was that dog at the gates of Hades?"

It was Cerberus, you bitch, thought Horacio, now shut up and untie me.

She prattled on. "As I was going into her house I thought I saw your amigo Beck, near the trailer here—although he was dressed down and had shaved his beard. I almost didn't recognize him, but I'm extremely visual. I'm an artist myself and see ten times more than most people."

Horacio noted that Sal wasn't visual enough to recognize the man she'd known for ten years as Horacio. To her he was only a Mexican laborer, hardly worth looking at as a person. That's why she felt comfortable blithering on to him. He was little more than a piece of furniture. But it was also clear Sal was in a bad way. Her mind, never particularly sharp, seemed to be deteriorating. Of course Horacio's own mind wasn't anything to brag about at this point. He wished she'd clam up and untie him, but he was damned if he was going to say por favor again.

Maybe because he was bored to death, Horacio again fell asleep.

28 IN THE HOUSE

JEFF RETURNED TO JENNY'S HOUSE.

Jenny embraced him happily, glad that he hadn't run off with the money and that she'd been right in her heart about him. His true affection and desire for her must have surpassed any temptation the money might have exerted. "Have you got the paintings?"

"They're at Pack 'n' Ship. That's where the thieves left them, ready to go to Paris. I drove over, checked that they were all there, and gave them the go-ahead to send them."

"Well, we have to stop them at once. There isn't any show. I think Beck just set me up to get the paintings for the ransom. He's a crook."

She made the call. "Don't send off those paintings to Paris. We'll be right down to get them." There was a pause as she listened, then exclaimed, "Oh no!"

She clicked off the phone and told Jeff, "They've gone." Then she told him about her call to Paris and of Sal's shocking confession.

He was unsurprised but did not say I told you so. "I just saw Sal wandering over to that trailer on the next lot. Why do you suppose she's gone there?"

"I have no idea. How strange."

"I still think she's involved in all this."

"No, she just suffered a lapse of integrity. She was attacked by the thief, Jeff!" A thought struck her. "What if the person who stole the paintings was really just trying to keep them from being destroyed? Now that's the sort of thing Horacio would do."

"Was he a crook?"

"No." Jenny did not want to tell Jeff about Horacio's secret life—only Gram knew about that. "Just unconventional. Went his own way. Made his own rules. A nonconformist." She got carried away. "But he was good-hearted, loyal. And brave."

Jeff looked grim. Trying to reassure him, Jenny said, "But I love you. It's early to talk about love, and I know we don't have a future. I'm too old to get married and have children and I'm sure you'll want those things. But, well, I thought you might like to know."

"Why didn't you have a child with Horacio?"

"He already had four. And Mae came to live with us, don't forget. She was like a daughter to me and still is." Jenny moved closer to Jeff. "Should we make love right now this minute? I feel like it will take away the strain."

"I have a life, you know," Jeff flared. "I have a job. Right this minute I'm supposed to be taking a picture of some sewing bee to make my ten-fucking-fifty an hour. And I'm hoping to get a ride in before this evening when the dog owners are holding a walk-in against the child soccer players who are taking their dog exercise area away from them. The children are sick of slipping in shit. I have to photograph this dynamic occasion for the paper. They'll all be long-legged golden dogs, of course. In this town, small dark dogs need not apply. Stumpy-legged bassets will be shot on sight. And I don't make love on command."

"Hardly a command," she laughed. Jenny noticed he was getting a hard-on just talking about it. And she was, too, or whatever was comparable: a soft-in, a meltdown.

"One gets hard, the other gets soft. It's such a perfect arrangement," she said. She stepped out of her linen pants and pulled down her lace panties. "We'll be quick."

Jeff pulled off his jeans and sat down in the armchair. "Sit on me," he said gruffly. "This way at least I get to sit down for a minute." Jenny was offended but felt lusty enough to comply. Even with no foreplay, even with his grudging acceptance of her suggestion, she was wildly excited. She liked the feeling of slipping down over him instead of his entering her. The initial penetration was her favorite part of intercourse—it took her breath away. It was the most consciously exciting part. After that she lost discrimination and became all sensation.

He eased forward so she could wrap her legs around the small of his back. "Who moves?" she asked, wondering how to proceed. They were locked fast together.

"No one moves." He was still talking gruffly. "Squeeze me with your insides." She did. He moved slightly with small quick thrusts then simply rested inside her, swelling, reaching upward, feeling his way. She imagined some fat sensitive tentacle inside her, questing along for her secret spots. It was all working out just fine. Then he put his hands under her rump and pulled her closer in, though Jenny had thought they could get no closer. He moved her up and down. She lolled her head over his shoulder. "You've got a minute to come, then I'm out of here."

"Are you going to come, too?"

"Of course."

"How long do you get to come?"

"I'm waiting for you."

This had not been idle conversation—it had come out in grunts and gasps and ended quite suddenly in mutual screams.

Afterwards Jeff was no longer in a hurry and stayed another hour with Jenny, being playful and affectionate rather than gruff. As he was leaving, Jenny walked out with him and they saw that Sal's car was still there. They looked toward the trailer, mystified. "I better go over there," Jeff said. "See what's up. Look, there seems to be a slight trail from here to there. Had you noticed that before?"

"It must be Abraham's. He's always going over that way." Abraham, hearing his name, appeared at Jenny's side and, when Jeff started over to the trailer, which was only a football field away over rough ground, went with him.

Jenny, noticing Abraham's zigzag approach, wondered if it was a man-made trail after all, or possibly a deer trail—they were more direct than dogs. She considered following them, but Jeff hadn't invited her to come and she didn't want to be a tagalong. Also, she didn't want to see Sal—maybe not ever again. At least not for a couple of weeks. Also, she wanted to lie down and read, maybe sleep. She wondered when she would get to paint again. How long had it been?

The sky was almost painfully blue, the sun still high. The days were getting longer. Poppies and lupin had appeared on the hill as if overnight, as if in the last hour. Down by the road, Acacia trees laden with yellow blossoms colored the dirt beneath them with pollen and petals. A California jay squawked at her from the roof. Abraham and Jeff grew small in the distance and were swallowed by chaparral. Jenny went back into the house.

A strange man was sitting in the coitus chair, waiting for her.

29 ALIVE

HARRY WAS NERVOUS. He asked himself what he wanted. If Jenny had been the one who'd nearly killed him, and his returning memory convinced him of it, did he want to kill her in revenge? He didn't think he had that brutal edge anymore. It was discouraging. He thought too much about things—like he was doing now.

He'd always had trouble with Jenny. She had what in the old days was called sex appeal. This combined with her femininity, innocence, and quirky personality was captivating. Both Jeff and Horacio were enthralled by her and Harry supposed that he was too. Except that he didn't get to sleep with her.

He had stolen half a million from her, which was satisfying, and he had a plan to get the other half. A million dollars for a week's work was all right. But what it came down to was that Jenny didn't care about the money. No, the best way to hurt Jenny would be to hurt Horacio—to kill him instead of her. Of course, Jenny couldn't be hurt by Horacio's death unless she knew he was still alive. But he couldn't tell her that convincingly until he told her that he, Harry, a.k.a. Laveen, was alive.

When Jenny walked in and saw him sitting in the chair, she reacted quickly, went right to the phone on the kitchen counter and punched 911. "I have an intruder," she said before Harry could reach her although he leapt with alacrity from the chair. He had not counted on this, thinking he could paralyze her with his unexpected presence in her home—although it was typical of Jenny to make an unforeseen move.

"No, Jenny," he said. "It's me. You know me. It's—it's Beck," he said, deciding to wait on the Huntington angle. "I shaved. We need to talk."

"Never mind," Jenny said to the police, "I was mistaken. It's someone I know who changed his appearance. A Mr. Harry Beck," she said for the record, making Harry want to strangle her. "It alarmed me." Harry wanted to alarm her more by breaking the connection. She continued talking. "This man has mistreated me in a business way so I will keep the phone handy in case things get nasty. Thanks. Good-bye."

She looked stonily at Harry. "You have some explaining to do."

He removed his dark glasses and showed what his glance could do. Jenny thought it was probably the same menacing look he'd given Jeff, along with the *fuck you* that Jeff kept practicing with such poor results. It made Jenny's blood run cold. She almost pressed redial. She hoped Jeff would come back here after checking out the trailer and not simply drive downtown to his sewing bee picture. She was sure it wasn't really a sewing bee. It was just his mocking way of talking about his job. Just as he said everyone's dog was a golden retriever, when actually, since the O.J. trial, there had been a burgeoning dog population of Akitas—for those people who didn't want a watchdog that would save their life, but one that would cry a lot afterward and wander disconsolately around the neighborhood. Anyhow, Jeff's presence would sure be a comfort right now, even though Harry scared Jeff more than he did her. She was scared right now but damned if she would show it.

"Please sit down," she said. "Let's talk." They both chose straight-back chairs and sat facing each other about four feet apart, as if they were going to play chess but had forgotten the table.

"I do have some explaining to do, Jenny. I'll start with who I am. I'm Horacio's cousin, Harry Huntington. You knew me, ten years ago, as Laveen. I'm alive."

Jenny stood up and clasped her hands to her breast. The telephone dropped from her lap to the floor. "This is absolutely wonderful!"

Harry's jaw dropped with amazement but he quickly closed it.

"You can't imagine what grief it has been to me to think that I had killed you, inadvertently though it was. I felt like a murderer, beyond redemption. Horacio helped me to deal with it over the years, but it has been terribly hard, knowing that I took a man's life, even though he was so evil and would have thought nothing of killing us all." Jenny had added this last part over the years to justify herself and she added it aloud now, forgetting that the evil incarnate was sitting in front of her, alive and listening. "How did you survive?"

Jenny sat down again as Harry told her how he'd awakened in the hills with amnesia. He had been able to make his way down to the road, where someone found him and drove him to a hospital. He had gone to France, the Dordogne, to begin a new life. Gradually his memory returned—all except the final trauma, so he had resolved to return to California and find Horacio. That was when he had read in the paper about Horacio's death and Jenny's inheritance. Harry had forgotten about her existence until then. Since seeing her, the remainder of his memory of his near death had come back to him.

"I had amnesia for a while too," said Jenny. "My memory of killing you only came back to me when I found the painting."

"What became of that painting?"

Again Jenny got to her feet and moved around the room as she talked. "Horacio and I gave it to a museum where we visited it every now and then. In the future of course, I'll have to visit it alone. But that will be nice, since I have no grave to go to for Horacio. I can go to the picture that brought us together. Horacio was the love of my life, you know."

"Bullshit. There is no such thing."

"Oh yes there is. Maybe you doubt me because of Jeff. But you see, Horacio and I hadn't lived together for over a year. Not that I need to explain anything to you. Let us move on to the business of the faux show."

"No, I want to talk about Horacio. He is still alive."

"No, he isn't."

"Believe me, he is. For now."

"Absolutely not. I wanted to think so but now I have trained myself to admit he is dead. Of course it's possible that his specter is floating around. It would be so like Horacio to leave a restless ghost crossing our paths now and then to keep us on our toes."

"His specter bleeds, then."

"I don't understand."

"Ask your new boyfriend. He tangled with Horacio this morning when he was trying to run off with your money. Horacio took it away from him."

She paled, sinking into her chair. "You're lying," Jenny said. "Horacio is dead and I bet it's you who has the money. Let's go look in your car."

"I do have the money and I have Horacio, and I'm going to kill him unless you do exactly as I say."

30 SUFFERING MEXICAN

JEFF STEPPED UP through the open door of the trailer. Sal was inside, sitting at the table, her head resting on her folded arms. On the bed was a man, tied up, snoring.

"What's going on?"

Sal looked up listlessly. "I'm waiting for Beck. I figure he's the one who tied up this man so he'll probably be back. I saw him over here when I came to Jenny's house earlier."

Jeff sat down at the table across from Sal.

Horacio, hearing voices, opened one eye and groaned. Now in his trailer were two people who he had recently knocked unconscious.

What about his privacy? Didn't people understand that a trailer was also a home, that you didn't just walk in and sit down? He wouldn't be surprised if they set about raiding his refrigerator.

"I figure he's tied up for a good reason," said Sal. "He's a Mexican."

"Maybe I should be tied up too," said Jeff. "I'm a Jew."

"I'm an Italian," said Sal.

"You should definitely be tied up," Jeff said.

"I should be. I should be tarred and feathered for what I almost did to Jenny's paintings. I suppose she told you," she added gloomily.

"Yes."

"But I was slugged and wrapped up and left at the side of the road. Maybe that's punishment enough."

"No, it's not. Anyhow, it probably didn't happen."

"You don't believe me?"

"No."

"Does Jenny believe me?"

"Yes."

"But you tried to tell her differently."

"Right."

"Bastard. But don't think I haven't tried to warn her about you—that you're only after her money. I'm amazed you didn't run off with the ransom money. I told her you would."

"Thanks."

"She didn't believe me. She's so loyal."

"I love Jenny."

"Bullshit."

"I'm crazy about her. I want her to have my baby."

The Mexican gave a jerk and groaned.

"Oh, sure," Sal said.

"Horacio wouldn't let her have a baby, you know. Mr. Perfect figured he had enough children already."

Unfair! thought Horacio, suppressing another groan. He and Jenny had never even talked about children. Her paintings were her children. He would have been glad to have babies with her. He loved kids. Well, maybe he groused about them sometimes, but who didn't? And Mae was like their daughter. Jenny had Mae, didn't she?

Abraham walked up the steps and through the door. He took in the situation then moseyed to the bed. Lifting his forepaws onto it, he began licking Horacio's wound.

"How sweet," said Sal, who had feared more snarls aimed at her. "But you know, that's the first time I've ever seen Abraham do that?"

"What, lick a wound?"

"No, put his feet on the furniture. He had a deal with Horacio, you know. Horacio would feed him if Abraham didn't get on the furniture. And Abraham said okay as long as he didn't ever have to wag his tail."

"I'm sick of hearing about Horacio and his cute Abraham stories."

"The fact is, Horacio was the love of Jenny's life, so you're going to have to live with it. The million dollars will help."

Horacio was wondering if dog drool was good for wounds. The licking didn't feel all that great but he was touched. Abraham didn't care if he was a Mexican.

He shifted his position so the dog could reach the ropes. Abraham obligingly began to gnaw at them. He was good at this, from the days when Horacio had had the nerve to try to tether him outside. He was also gnawing on Horacio's wrists while he was at it but that was okay.

"Look what Abraham's doing now," Sal said.

"Abraham, cut it out," Jeff snapped.

"He only obeys Horacio, and not even him all the time," said Sal, dog historian.

Jenny suddenly walked in the trailer. Abraham stopped what he was doing, put his paws back on the floor, and walked the few steps to greet her. "What on earth?" she exclaimed.

Oh no! thought Horacio. *Madre de diós! Caramba!*

"Look at that poor man! Why are you just sitting here while he's suffering?" She went at once to release him.

Horacio had been on his stomach so that Abraham could get to the ropes. Now he buried his face in the pillow as Jenny sat on the bed next to him.

It was amazing how everyone was wandering into his trailer. Where was Mae? he wondered. Why wasn't Gram here? It was lucky the door was open or they'd run out of oxygen. At least Harry hadn't returned. That was a good thing.

"We didn't think we should interfere," Sal answered.

"But what right do you have to even be in this man's home?"

See, Jenny knows it's a home, thought Horacio. Jenny was wonderful.

"I was looking for Beck," Sal explained.

"Beck's been at my house. Look at this horrible gash on the back of his head." Jenny took charge. "Jeff, please go to the medicine cabinet. He must have some bandages and ointment there. Working men are always getting hurt. Sal, get out of here. I don't want to see you." Jenny walked to the sink and soaped up a wet cloth. She returned to the bed and began daubing Horacio's wound, which hurt much more than Abraham's method.

"But I was going to try to talk Beck back into the show."

"Forget it," said Jenny. "There's not a chance."

"But—"

Abraham remembered his job and growled at Sal, who quickly departed. As Jenny dressed Horacio's wound, he dug his face deeper into the pillow to hide from her, but had to periodically come to the pillow's surface to breathe. She untied his wrists. His hands were numb. She asked how he was feeling.

He lifted his chin from the pillow enough to say, "*Muy bien, gracias. Mucho mejor que antes. Adiós.*" He stressed the *adiós*.

"He wants us to go, Jeff."

As they went out the door, Horacio heard Jenny say, "I've got to talk to you. Beck wants the other half million for Horacio."

"I hope you told him to dream on. Does he think we're complete idiots?"

"He's going to kill him, Jeff!"

"Horacio's already dead. I won't even discuss this."

"I know Beck's just trying to get more money out of us. But what if Horacio isn't dead? Beck said Horacio was the man who took the money from you this morning."

They were walking slowly down the path so Horacio strained to hear them.

"I wouldn't know. He had a gun on my back and wouldn't let me turn around."

Now they must have stopped to talk because their voices weren't getting smaller.

"Do you think it could have been Horacio?" Jenny asked.

"No I don't. Forget it. Forget him."

“If Beck can prove to me Horacio’s alive, and in danger, then I’m giving the money. That’s all there is to it.”

“We’re not giving that crook another red cent. Horacio’s already dead. If he’s twice dead, who cares?”

“I care. How can you be so unfeeling?”

“If Horacio is alive, he’s in on this scheme and is trying to get his money back from you, God knows for what twisted motive, and you should just tell Beck no deal. He’s not going to kill his own partner.”

“There’s a lot you don’t know.”

“If it’s about Horacio, I don’t want to know.”

Now the voices dwindled away.

Horacio yearned for Jenny. He thought of her gentle touch as she tended to his wound, the tremble in her fingers. Poor Jenny had always hated blood. It was a wonder she hadn’t keeled over beside him, digging her face into the pillow beside him.

Would her head ever again lie next to his? It didn’t look like it would. But right now he had to defuse the situation.

He rubbed his hands together until his fingers were able to untie his ankles. The gun had been taken from his work belt, but the phone was still there. He called a taxi and told him where to wait. Then he put some things in a pack: his Vietnam book, the cowboy boots, some T-shirts and briefs, his shaving kit, and the rope he’d been tied with. He turned off the gas, took a last look around, walked out the door and locked it.

He didn’t take his usual path but ran up and over the hill, which took him to a different residential part of town. Here, as instructed, the taxi was waiting.

Horacio got in and said, “Airport.”

31 JENNY THINKS THINGS OVER

THE REASON JENNY HAD TALKED to Jeff outside the trailer was to warn Horacio. She had known him as soon as she began to bathe his wound. Despite his hidden face. Just as a holograph of the whole body can be made from a man's little finger, so could she conjure Horacio from the way his hair grew at the back of his head, or from the way his jawline met his ear. And of course she knew him by his hands, which were captured motionless before her eyes as she worked on the ropes. Large, gnarled, and work-worn though they were, he always kept them scrupulously clean, and his nails nice. She knew every vein and knuckle. She knew the lines in his palm. She knew his flesh. With her eyes closed, she could touch his skin and know it was his.

Although her heart was singing that Horacio was alive, there was much that she didn't understand and much more that she was angry with him about. She wished she could have cleared the trailer of Jeff as well as Sal and torn into him about his outrageous behavior, but the main thing now was to keep him safe from Harry, and keep herself safe too. If she had to give Harry the rest of the money, she would. Clearly she should never have accepted it to begin with. She had sold out.

But never mind. Horacio was alive—and so was Harry. That was such a load off her heart and soul. No one in the world, except Horacio and Gram, knew she had killed a man, and it had been a burden almost too hard to carry. Now that she knew he was alive she could hope that he hadn't returned to his life of evil. Maybe what he was doing now to her was only vengeance and he would be appeased by the money.

To think that Horacio, all this time, had been the man next door, the man in the tree, invading her silence with his air-splitting saw, obviously the man who had broken into her house and knocked out Jeff. No wonder Abraham was always going off in that direction. She remembered how Jeff had said the dog had watched the fight, smiling and wagging his tail, and she had to smile to herself. She understood about the kimono now, too.

Yes, she thought soberly, it must have been hard for Horacio to see her take the money and take Jeff too. Maybe Horacio had thought he was demonstrating to her how much she loved him by having her irremediably lose him. And then Harry had shown up. She shivered just thinking about him.

Now Jenny was in bed. Jeff had gone to take his pictures for the *Mill Valley News,* then to his bike ride and dinner with his buddies. In the morning she would have to talk to him some more about the ransom money. She hoped that Horacio, once free, had gotten free from Harry too, but as long as she didn't know for sure she would have to pay the money. That was okay. She would be glad to be rid of it—but Jeff wouldn't be.

She wondered if she should tell Jeff that Horacio was alive. Would he believe her if she said he was the man in the trailer? He hadn't believed her the other times she expressed her doubts about his death, getting angry with her each time and refusing to listen. She hadn't exposed Horacio at the time she was nursing his wound because if Horacio still wanted to be thought dead, she had to respect his wishes. She knew that if she had tried to expose him, he would have gone on playing the Mexican to the limit and Sal and Jeff would have just thought she was nuts.

It was easier to pretend around Jeff that Horacio was dead, and easier vis-à-vis Horacio that he didn't know she knew he was alive. He would be so humiliated to have her find him hog-tied in his little trailer—Horacio, the daring, dashing jewel thief, lord of his twenty-room mansion, Horacio the strong and indestructible. Yes, it had been a sad sight. He would rather be thought dead than recognized in such a pitiful position.

Jenny laughed sleepily. Soon, though, her thoughts turned to Sal and she grew wakeful and grim, remembering Sal's appalling confession. Jenny had never wanted to see her again. But then, later, when she'd entered the trailer and seen Sal sitting there, looking so distraught, so bedraggled, it gave Jenny's heart a pang.

It was maddening to feel the slightest sympathy for Sal. If Sal was feeling bad about her actions, she was supposed to! That's what guilt was for.

But it was hard to remain angry with someone who was so clearly penitent and who was trying, however stupidly, to right the wrong. Jenny supposed she would have to forgive Sal, that being knocked out and left on the road—as well as being growled at twice by Abraham—was punishment enough. And Sal was punishing herself by continuing to wear the dirty, torn, wrinkled, linen and silk outfit when she normally changed clothes three or four times a day. It was a way to flag her ordeal. Jenny had to be glad that she wasn't wearing the air bag around too. She dreaded seeing Sal again and finding her still in the same clothes.

Early the next morning, while Jeff was still sleeping, she rose, got dressed and, with Abraham, followed Horacio's narrow path to the trailer. Now it was her turn to snoop.

Jenny hoped Horacio was still in there. Just let him try to pretend to be a Mexican when it's just the two of us, she thought. She'd rip off his shirt and point to every scar she knew by heart. Come to think of it, she could rip off his ear.

Horacio was gone. The trailer was locked and the curtains pulled. Abraham sniffed around and took off over the hill but Jenny was not about to go cross country in search of him. Was Horacio with Harry, or had he bolted?

Back home, she checked that Jeff was still asleep then called Harry.

"Where do things stand this morning?" she asked.

"Nothing has changed. I have Horacio. You have the money. Let's trade."

"Let me talk to him. I want proof that he's alive."

Harry said, "I have one sentence I'm allowing him to repeat, nothing more. I have a gun on him."

Jenny heard Horacio's voice say, "There are some things it's best never to know."

"Horacio!" Jenny shouted into the phone.

"That's all he's saying." Harry was back on the line.

"That's Horacio's voice all right but—why can't I see him?"

"He doesn't want to see you." Jenny was silent, thinking this was probably true.

"How do I know you'll let him go after I give you the money?"

"I'm sure he'll get in touch with you. I myself am returning to France this afternoon."

Jenny wished she could find out if Horacio was in on this scheme with his cousin, or if he was in real danger.

"Let me hear his voice again."

Harry hesitated, then refused. They bickered for several minutes until Harry decided to oblige.

Again Horacio said, "There are some things it's best never to know." It sounded the same as before.

She listened intently. It could easily be a recording. She was pretty sure she heard a click afterward. Certainly his inflection was identical both times—but that wouldn't be unusual for Horacio.

Even if he weren't there with Harry, she had to proceed as if he were. She would pay the ransom even though it would leave her poorer than before because of all the new bills, and even though she was ignoring Jeff's injunction not to give Harry another red cent.

"Where should I take the money?"

Harry gave her instructions. Then she made coffee and squeezed orange juice, which she took on a tray to the bedroom.

She would talk with Jeff one last time about the situation and try to get his blessing on paying the ransom. Without revealing that she'd already said yes to Harry. She set down the tray, drew the curtain, then got into bed beside him.

32 JEFF THINKS THINGS OVER

JEFF WAS AWAKENED by Jenny snuggling next to him. She'd brought him a mug of coffee. This was a nice way to wake up. It beat the hell out of the head-banging system. The accommodations weren't luxurious, but they were nice. The bed was comfortable, the view of the mountain was splendid, and he really did like Jenny. If they could just clear up this Horacio mess, it would be smooth sailing.

His thoughts had started to clear yesterday while photographing the angry dog owners, whose exercise field was to be plowed into a soccer field. He had begun to think about the acrimonious undercurrents in this town of nice, intelligent, successful, privileged people where dog owners fought with kid owners, hikers fought with bikers, neighborhoods were at war over traffic patterns being funneled from one to the other. He thought of the wrathful faces he'd photographed at the town meeting and he thought what a good book they would make—the photos of this ostensibly idyllic town with its raging mini-wars.

The stupid small-town pictures he hated taking, when put together, made a hell of a big picture of how, even in an ideal living situation, men and women will turn on each other. You don't have to be a different religion or color, you only have to live on a different street, ride a bike, or have a dog to want to tear the other person limb from limb. People seemed to need trouble and anger in their lives and could create it out of nothing.

For the first time in years, Jeff felt like getting to work. Maybe it was his time with Jenny that had fired him up. Her discipline and love of work was inspiring him. It was lucky he hadn't got away with the money yesterday. That had been a close call. He might be a wanted criminal now instead of having coffee brought to him in bed by a loving woman.

When Jeff's father had shot him down by saying his Pulitzer was due to a lucky break, being in the right place at the right time, he'd believed him enough to feel he'd have to take some other route to impress him. Now he knew the way to prove himself as a photographer, to show he had real merit.

Ideally he should commit himself to the task for his own sake, not to prove his worth to his father, but that liberating day would probably never come.

Jenny interrupted his thoughts. "How do you feel this morning about my paying Harry the ransom money for Horacio?"

"I've never been more against anything in my life."

"I have to say, Jeff, that I believe Horacio is alive. It's not just my imagination."

Jeff knew it too. But that didn't change anything because he didn't care about him. If Horacio was supposed to be dead, then let him be dead. If Jeff was signing the guy's death warrant by not telling Jenny he was alive, then so be it. It was all in the abstract. It didn't make Jeff a murderer—he was just looking out for himself.

"If he's alive, he got himself into this mess—let him get himself out. If he's alive, he's probably playing footsie with Harry. I gather they go way back. Didn't you say that they're cousins?"

"Yes, but . . . you see—"

"Spare me the history. I think he's dead and Harry's jerking you around."

"Does the money matter that much to you?"

"What matters to me is your being played for a fool. I don't want to live with a fool. Up until now I've admired you more than any woman I've known."

"How nice. But are you saying that you'll stop admiring me? You won't want to live with me anymore?" Her big eyes gazed on him thoughtfully.

"That's what I'm saying."

Jeff knew that Jenny could interpret this as him not wanting her without the money. He didn't think she'd ask him outright even though Sal had tried to convince her of that fact. Jenny was too proud, too loyal, too loving, and too innocent. She believed what she wanted to believe, which was that her money didn't have anything to do with his feelings for her.

"Do you love me because of the money?" she asked outright.

"I never said I loved you," he reminded her, smiling.

"That's right," she responded seriously. "It was I who said I love you."

Jeff felt Jenny slipping away from him so he said something he thought was charming. "Disraeli said to his wife when she was dying, 'I married you for your money, but if I had it to do over again, I'd marry you for love.' She was also about ten years older than he was, like us." Jeff smiled and sipped his coffee.

"So? What's the message here?"

He decided to hang tough. It's what she liked about him. He'd never been smarmy and he wasn't going to start now. "The message is, if you give Beck the rest of the money, I'm out of here."

She flushed, then quietly asked, "Even if it means Horacio dying?"

"You know where I stand on that. I don't want to talk about it anymore. It's up to you." Jeff decided to go a step further and make it clear who was calling the shots. "And if I stay here with you, I don't want to hear the name Horacio again." He would have liked to add, "and we get rid of the dog," but had the good sense to know that would be going too far.

Jenny looked shaken. He supposed he better fuck her to drive the point home. He put his coffee mug down and addressed himself to the task. She was stiff and uninclined at first, but with his patient kisses and slow hands, she soon became soft and willing, then eagerly responsive—as usual.

33 ADVICE

AN HOUR LATER, after Jeff had left for the day, Jenny called Gram to fill her in on everything that had happened, including her latest conversation with Jeff. "I'm going to go ahead and give the ransom money to Harry," she said.

"Of course," Gram agreed.

"But I'm not going to tell Jeff. I don't want to lose him, Gram."

"Don't you think he'll find out when there's no money available for those extras he seems so fond of."

"Yes, but I figure I'll have a couple of weeks before it all blows up in my face. Those weeks will be worth it."

"I understand, darling. An impassioned and satisfying sexual relationship is something to honor. I know—I've had one or two in my life I wouldn't have forsworn for anything, no matter what sort of wreckage they subsequently caused. But, as uplifting as such an affair is, the day comes when you begin to feel demoralized, when you reckon that your character is being changed for the worse and that, by virtue of your insatiable yearning, you are allowing yourself to be abused. That's the day you must end it."

"I don't think of this as just an affair. I feel that Jeff and I could have a future together."

"I thought I heard you say you've got two weeks. Is that a future?"

"Gram, when you came here for the night, you said that if you'd known I was in trouble, you would have helped me out."

Gram laughed. "Yes, I did. So that's your plan? To get the money from me to disguise the fact you acted against your lover's wishes?"

"What do you think?"

"What's it going to cost me? I certainly can't pony up a million."

"How about four thousand a month and we'll see how it goes?"

"Happy to do it, Jenny."

"Thank you with all my heart."

"You know I want to leave you money when I die anyway. How much better to see you enjoy it while I'm alive."

"I will enjoy it. But don't mention death. I need you here on earth."

"Jenny, I have a suspicion four thousand won't be enough. Didn't I hear something about a swimming pool? A Jacuzzi? A weight room? A trip to France?"

"I don't think he really cares so much about the money. He just doesn't want me to be played for a fool. I suppose I am a fool to hand it all over to Harry but I can't let Horacio be killed."

"You're sure he's alive?"

"Positive."

"If I'd said no on helping you out, would you still go ahead and pay the ransom?"

"Of course! I've already arranged it with the bank. Please don't doubt me."

"It's only that this young man has such a hold on you."

"But I'm still my own person. You, Horacio, and Mae are still the most important people in my life. And Abraham. I'd do anything for any of you. You're my family."

"I know, sweetheart." Gram sighed. "How is your painting going?"

"It isn't. But after today, I'm back on schedule, and back to my daily hikes, too, which I sorely miss. Tomorrow all this craziness will be over."

"Good. I'll arrange for my bank to wire money to your account each month. Give me your account number."

Jenny did so and they bid each other adieu. Then she took her big battered old Random House dictionary and looked up *demoralize.*

"To deprive a person of spirit, courage, discipline," she read. "To destroy the morale of, throw into disorder or confusion, to corrupt or undermine the morals of."

I think I'm okay so far, she thought. But I can see how it would only be a step from demoralized to morally reprehensible. Because if you lose your courage and discipline, you have no base; you flounder about in a state of disorder and confusion, grasping at straws, having no sense of who you are or of what is right or wrong.

But it seemed to Jenny that even during the worst of her crazy spells, the most disordered of her nervous breakdowns, the times she was most scared and undisciplined, she still kept her moral sense. She had never been a corrupt person or a reprehensible person although there is no getting around the fact that she had tainted herself by taking that money and so brought all this trouble down on her head.

She suddenly realized that she'd forgotten to tell Mae her father was alive.

As if on Jenny's wavelength, Mae appeared fifteen minutes later.

They hugged each other, then Jenny sat her down and filled her in on the developments regarding the stolen paintings. "They're on their way to Paris, but there will be no show; it was all a hoax."

Mae hugged Jenny. Sitting at the kitchen counter, she listened to the details while she painted her nails silver. Jenny stood, leaning on the counter, sometimes pacing the kitchen. Periodically she paused in her narration, entranced by Mae's swift sure strokes. She'd never been able to paint her own nails without making a mess of it which was strange since she was such a careful and controlled painter of canvasses. She went on to tell about the visit to the trailer.

"Wait a minute," interrupted Mae. "Let me give you a manicure, too."

She filled a bowl with soapy water for Jenny to soak her nails, then took scissors, cotton, orange sticks, and a file from her shoulder bag. "At least you don't have paint all over your hands for once." She flashed the file over Jenny's nails, making a nice edge. "Why don't you, by the way?"

"I haven't painted for a few days." It was the longest she'd gone in her life.

While she was getting manicured, Jenny told Mae how she had discovered Horacio. She led up to it gradually because unlike Jenny, she had grieved and moved on.

"First Sal went over to the trailer, thinking she'd seen Beck go that way and wanting to persuade him to go on with the show. He really does have a gallery. We checked. After a while, when she didn't return, Jeff and Abraham followed her over, and when they didn't return, I followed them."

Jenny paused to enjoy the luxury of the manicure. Mae laughed and said, "It must have been like one of those circus cars full of clowns."

Jenny went on.

"The Mexican who has been clearing the land for the building project was there, lying on the bed, with a wound on the back of his head. I took care of him. And Mae, this may come as a shock, but the Mexican was your Dad. It was Horacio."

Mae stopped, the tiny brush poised in the air, looking at Jenny with her big eyes. "No!"

"Yes. Really. It's true."

Mae screwed the brush back into the polish bottle. Then she put her hands on Jenny's shoulders. "Oh, Mom, poor you. You miss him so much, I'm afraid now you have imagined the Mexican into being him."

"Mae, it was him. I know it's hard—"

"Did he say anything?"

"Well, no—"

"Did you say something?"

"No. You know Horacio. He would have denied it and turned himself inside out being even more Mexican. He probably would have started singing "Besame Mucho." He'd dyed his hair black, grown it long, and had a drooping Viva Zapata mustache."

Mae shook her head. "It sure doesn't sound as if he looked much like my Dad."

"I would know Horacio even if I just saw his little finger." Jenny suddenly felt like crying. She wanted Mae to believe her, but she could understand her not wanting to get her hopes up. Jenny wiped away the tears with her sleeve, surprised at how wet it became.

"Isn't it true that you've been imagining everyone is Horacio?" Mae asked gently, putting away the manicure kit. "Didn't you think that guy Beck was him at first?"

"Yes, sort of, but—"

"I don't know, Mom. You definitely have a problem here. Jeff told me how you're always saying you think Horacio's alive, and how it pisses him off. He says you're always looking over your shoulder like he's here in the house somewhere."

"But he has been here. Don't you see? He's been living right next door in that trailer. There's a path from there to here—I think he's been snooping around the whole time. You know how he can move like a cat."

Mae closed her eyes. She didn't believe Jenny.

"When did Jeff tell you that?" Jenny asked.

"I saw him last night with his bicycle buddies eating at the Italian place. I think he's hot for you, Mom. And I think he's jealous of Dad, dead or alive."

"Mae, I know it's hard for you to grasp, but your father is alive. However, the trailer is locked up today so I think he's gone."

"He is long gone," Mae insisted.

Jenny ignored her. "I think he left because he knew I guessed it was him."

"I doubt it. He always used to sucker you. You never knew when he was pulling a joke on you. Remember when he used to fall down on the ground and have those fits? Rolling around, frothing at the mouth. I always wondered how he worked up the froth." Mae laughed. "You got taken in every time. Remember the time you tried to get hold of his tongue so he wouldn't swallow it?" She howled with laughter.

Jenny felt abashed. "He was good at those fits all right. It's certainly nice to be with a normal person now."

"I personally don't think there's any such thing as a normal person. At least I haven't met it personified in any male."

"What do you think of Jeff?"

"You really want to know? I wouldn't trust him as far as I could throw him."

Jenny remembered Harry saying Jeff would have taken the ransom money if Horacio hadn't stopped him. She hadn't believed Harry, because at that point she didn't know that Horacio was living next door. And she still wasn't going to take Harry's word about anything. Nor Mae's for that matter. What did Mae know about Jeff?

"Don't look so glum. It doesn't mean you can't enjoy Jeff and have fun with him. Just don't invest too much is all. I don't want you to get hurt, Mom."

"Thanks, honey."

So Gram thought she'd get demoralized and Mae thought she'd get hurt. It didn't look like too bright a future. But maybe Jeff would prove them all wrong.

"You know what you need?" Mae said. "A mountain hit. Let's go for a hike. This is my last day of vacation. Come on."

"Great idea. I just have to do one teeny errand downtown." The teeny errand was taking five hundred thousand dollars from seven banks to the Mill Valley Inn.

"I'm in no hurry. It's lounge time." Mae wandered out onto the deck. Jenny changed into the green suit she'd worn the day Jeff bicycled her down the hill.

It seemed so long ago, but it was only a week. What a week it had been. A million dollars had come into her hands and slipped through her fingers.

But still, she'd rather lose her money than spend her life being afraid of losing it, distrusting everyone in her path. It was wonderful how without fear she was these days. Although the perfect thing would be to be fearless and have the money too.

34 SHOWDOWN

HARRY WAS FURIOUS when he returned to the trailer and found Horacio gone. He knew Horacio didn't have a car, so he checked with Mill Valley Taxi and discovered they'd picked up someone of Horacio's description yesterday afternoon. The driver had taken Horacio to San Francisco Airport. "What airline?"

"Long-term parking," the dispatcher answered.

Horacio's way of covering his tracks. He could grab a shuttle there to any airline. He was gone. It didn't matter. The ransom money was on the way. Jenny had been fooled by a bit from a tape he'd made secretly and had accepted it as Horacio's live voice. He wasn't going to have the pleasure of killing Horacio in front of Jenny, but that could wait for another time. Horacio would be back. He wouldn't leave Jenny alone for long—and he was hot to build a house on that million-dollar acreage next to Jenny's.

Harry returned to his room, changed into his gray traveling suit and packed his bags. At two o'clock, Jenny knocked on his door. He opened it, holding a gun close to his thigh. She stood there with a rattan bag. She was beautifully dressed in a suit the color of celadon, of an ancient oriental vase. Elegant. And she was self-contained. She'd come a long way since her days as a crazy girl.

"Come in."

"No. I'll just stand here while you check the money." She handed him the bag. "I took out ten thousand dollars to cover outstanding checks. My paintings have been shipped to Paris. I need to be assured you'll return them."

"I will." Harry took the bag inside and placed it on the bed near a large suitcase containing the rest of the money. Harry removed the stacks of bills from the rattan bag and placed them in the suitcase, counting it quickly as he did so.

"Where is Horacio?" she asked, leaning negligently against the doorjamb like a languid blade of grass.

"He's safe."

"Please tell him to send me some sort of message so I'll know he's okay."

"That's up to him. The truth is, he's gone. I don't know where he is. He took off."

"I'm glad he got away."

"Horacio's looking after his own hide."

"Good for him."

"He abandoned you with me still here in town preying on you. I'm surprised. He pictured himself as your protector."

"I can look after myself just fine. Don't forget, it was me who put you out of commission the last time, not Horacio."

"I did forget, for almost ten years, but now I've remembered. This trip, all in all, has been worthwhile."

"You have a chance to turn your life around. The police think you're dead. Why not live a decent life from now on?"

"Because it's boring."

"That was Horacio's excuse too. I don't understand it. Life is exciting to me just standing in front of my easel."

"You haven't tasted the kind of excitement that we have."

"Oh yes I have, and it tastes rotten."

"To each his own. You can have your dream world. I'll take the real world."

"Your world isn't real. It is artificial. You manufacture excitement and violence out of greed."

"It isn't the money; it's the game."

"Sure. That's what Horacio said too. 'To be on the wire is life. The rest is waiting.' It's sick. You're both sick. But he can inspire love."

Harry closed the suitcase and handed the rattan bag to Jenny. "I inspire fear. Unlike love, you can trust fear. No one pretends to be afraid. No one cheats with fear. I always know exactly where I stand. I have a plane to catch. Good-bye."

"Good-bye." Jenny eased away from the door and disappeared from view.

Harry closed the door and when he turned back to the room he noticed that one of the double doors of the armoire had opened a crack. He stood quietly. The gun was on the bed, closer to the armoire than to him. Possibly the door had come ajar on its own. He would like to make sure of the fact with the gun in his hand. He moved carefully toward the bed. Horacio burst out of the armoire. They both lunged for the gun. Harry knew he would lose in a physical fight with Horacio. He had to get the gun. He should never have set it down. Once again, Jenny had distracted him.

Harry got to the gun first, grabbed it, leapt back from the bed and pointed it at Horacio.

"Damn!" Horacio exclaimed. He sat on the bed. "Of course, I'm not at my best. Yesterday you bashed me on the head and two days before I had the fight with Jeff. My reactions have slowed."

"I believed you had left. That was good. You tricked me."

"You should have known I would never leave Jenny with you still around. But you don't understand those kind of feelings."

"Don't you start."

"It's true. You can't accurately judge people's behavior if you don't consider their emotions. It was a failure of reason on your part because of this blind spot of yours."

"Oh, shut up. I've got to figure out what to do with you now."

Horacio went on, "Jenny knows I wouldn't cut out on her."

"She believes you did cut out on her, and she's glad," Harry said angrily. "She doesn't need you anymore. She's fine with Jeff. And even without Jeff she doesn't want you any more. You heard her. She said you were sick."

"I am sick. I'm sick of life and of everyone in it—except Jenny. It's only because of her I didn't kill myself. Because she needs me."

"She doesn't need you!" Harry shouted. Why wouldn't Horacio get the message? Why did he so much want Horacio to get the message? "She doesn't need you or want you. She's glad you're gone. She's happy with Jeff. She thinks you're sick. Repeat all that to me."

Horacio was damned if he would repeat any of it. Harry was just worked up because the love he and Jenny had for each other was beyond his understanding.

"If that's true then kill me." Horacio lay down on the bed. "I've got nothing to live for. Good-bye, boring world. I thought it would be fun to see what Jenny did with the million, but it wasn't fun. Here." He held up a pillow. "Use this as a silencer."

"Good idea." When Harry came forward to get the pillow, Horacio flung another pillow at his face, catapulting himself upright and seizing the gun.

Horacio smiled. "If Jenny could see me now, maybe she'd begin to understand. She never really sees me in action, having fun. What a shame. It would be an eye-opener for her. I'm so good at it."

Harry asked tiredly, "What now?"

"Now, you call your Galerie La-fucking-Vigne and tell them the paintings are on their way and to go on with the show at the first opportunity. Tell them you don't know if you will be returning to France."

"You're a fool. No one is going to buy Jenny's paintings. You'll only humiliate her."

Horacio put the gun to Harry's temple. Harry said, "She's no good, Horacio. Face it."

"You're the one who's no good. All you know about art is what you read in books. You need a soul to discover an original new artist like Jenny. Pick up the phone." He cocked the gun.

Harry made the call.

"Now it's head meets gun-butt time. Turnabout is fair play, cousin."

Horacio was about to smash the gun against Harry's skull when Harry turned white as a sheet. Horacio was dismayed to see a legend scared out of his wits. It was like seeing Julius Caesar scared.

"No, no, not my head," Harry cried, stepping backwards. Unbalanced, he fell and cracked the very head he was trying to preserve against the fireplace mantle. He released a horrible "Aargh!" sound, part scream, part groan, and slumped to the floor.

Horacio took his rope from the armoire intending to hog-tie Harry. He hoped Harry would revive in time to see him walk away victoriously with the entire million. He bent over Harry who, even with his eyes open, wasn't going to see anything anymore.

"Whoa. Wait a minute." Horacio felt dizzy. He sat down on the bed, his head in his hands. "Harry, this wasn't in the plan." He looked up. "I'd better double check. I was wrong ten years ago." He looked around nervously. "Why am I talking out loud?"

There wasn't much blood but Harry was morbidly still. His eyes were open and glazed. That was a pretty sure sign that the curtains were drawn and the play was over. He checked for Harry's pulse and didn't find one.

He remembered Harry telling him that since the other accident, his skull was like an eggshell that had been pieced back together. That's why he was so scared of being struck. Horacio hadn't killed him, exactly, he'd only frightened him to death.

He remembered Jenny's mantra: "He was an evil man and deserved to die. He was going to kill us all," which she had used to assuage her guilt. The words rang hollow now.

Harry had lost his evil. He was no longer a mastermind. Nor did Horacio believe Harry had intended to kill him. He'd had opportunities and passed them by. Yesterday was a totally half-assed attempt at taking him prisoner. He could have gotten away any time he felt like it if he hadn't been so busy entertaining the neighborhood and taking naps.

Harry certainly wasn't a man of any heart but Horacio believed his cousin had nourished a smidgen of feeling for him, had liked him as well as he'd liked any man.

No, Harry wasn't the man he had been, and it was sad to see. Just as well he'd died in full action instead of becoming a querulous old man, boring people in bars with his exploits, showing up nightly in different disguises so as to show how he'd baffled people in his youth.

Horacio pulled himself together. Mourning was over. Three minutes was enough.

He stripped Harry of his clothes, changing outfits with him. He went through Harry's bags until he found the wig, beard, and glasses, and donned them.

He would sign out of the Mill Valley Inn as Harry Beck, and when the body was discovered it would be an unidentified person who had died accidentally.

Horacio carried the suitcase down to his Toyota Forerunner he'd recovered from the airport, where he left it after arriving from Mexico ten days ago, still covered in Mexican mud. It had been ten days of adventure, an emotional roller coaster that would last him for a while. It was safe to leave Jenny now, although he wished he could see her face when she heard that the Paris show was to go on. He wished he could see Jenny's face for any reason.

At least he'd gotten to hear her voice, to feel her trembling hands nurse his wound. Maybe that would be their last intimacy. It would depend on whether Jeff stuck around with the money gone. If he did, maybe it would prove he cared for Jenny after all.

Horacio checked out of the Mill Valley Inn, got in his truck, and headed south.

35 DEAD MAN

JEFF WAS AT THE NEWSPAPER OFFICE when the word came in about the body at the Mill Valley Inn. This was unprecedented—Mill Valley never had dead bodies in public places. Even the golden retrievers didn't die in public. He was dispatched to the scene with his camera. His pulse raced when he saw that it was Harry Beck's room. He couldn't cross the yellow police tape at the door, but he could see that the body wasn't Beck. Using a zoom lens, he took pictures. The paper wouldn't print them—this wasn't a bake sale—but he wanted to have them for himself. If it wasn't Beck, it could well be Horacio. If it was Horacio it was because Jenny hadn't paid the ransom—and she hadn't paid the ransom because he had forbidden it.

He thought he had better get Jenny out of town so she wouldn't hear the news, see it, or read it. He should never have bought a television. She was no longer isolated. He would suggest a romantic journey down the coast—if she stayed in town her remorse would be unassailable. The death of her ex would not reflect well upon him and his advice-giving powers. On the other hand Jeff wished she could know Horacio was dead. She had Horacio on the brain. He was a blight on their life together. Jeff was glad he would have the photos of the body for future proof. But for now it was better she didn't know.

Sal, still trying to corner Beck about Jenny's show, had gone to the Mill Valley Inn and been told he'd checked out. Fran, the woman at the desk, an acquaintance of Sal's, was quick to divulge the thrilling information regarding the unidentified dead body in Beck's room. Sal pressed her for details.

"There's been some guy in and out the whole time Mr. Beck was here, but it wasn't the dead man—it was a Mexican."

"Oh yes, the Mexican," Sal said, "I know about the Mexican, Beck's amigo."

"But the dead man was bald as a bean."

"Was he murdered?"

"I don't think so. At least, he wasn't shot or stabbed."

"I have to tell my friend Jenny Hunt. She knows Beck."

"Tall and thin? Sort of looks like Audrey Hepburn?"

"Well, yes. A boring Audrey Hepburn."

"She was here today. But, it was before Mr. Beck checked out. So, I guess she didn't do it. What happened to you, by the way? You look like something the cat dragged in."

"I was in an auto accident."

"Is that the air bag?"

"Yes."

"Cool. You could start a new fashion. Air bag chic. Still, I'd clean up if I were you. People might get the wrong impression."

"Maybe the wrong impression is the right one," Sal said. She turned on her heel and, head high, air bag flowing, sashayed out the door.

She climbed on her bicycle and wound her way up the hill to Jenny's house.

Jenny was painting. Or trying to paint. After hiking with Mae, she had gone to her studio with a high heart but when she uncovered Constellation, her masterpiece, it looked dead to her, flat, colorless. It didn't sing. The promise was gone. It looked juvenile, ill conceived, clumsily executed. It was as if in her absence someone had replaced her beautiful creation with this mockery, this bad reproduction, this distortion. Yes, it was as if each of its elements was slightly distorted, out of balance, their harmony destroyed. She could hardly bear to look at it.

She turned away, wringing her hands, trying to buoy herself up. When I get working on it, she told herself, it will come back into focus. The vision will fall into place. I've been away from it too long. All these distractions have put me off my stride. My life has undergone a major shift. I have to slow down, get back on schedule, make painting my first priority.

She squeezed some paint on her palette and set out the brushes she would need for Venus, which was to be Jeff's pupil and iris, lit from within. She covered her brush with green, raised it high, then stood immobile in front of the canvas, unable to lay on the merest speck of paint.

Her mind was full of everything but the painting before her. There was too much that was unresolved. Her mind had to be clear, but it was like a roiling river in there instead of a pristine pool. It was hopeless to try to paint now, at the end of such a tempestuous day. She would try again tomorrow, right after breakfast.

Jenny covered her palette with saran wrap to keep the paint that was on it from drying out. With turpentine, then soap and water, she cleaned the brush of its green tint. She threw the sheet over the canvas and stood there.

She was tempted to destroy the half-done work. What if she died and this was all that was left of her work to show the world, this mess in masterpiece's clothing? She would hate to be remembered for this.

She was swept by a feeling of meaninglessness, of nothing to do and nothing to hope for. For a few seconds the bottom fell out of her life. The thought of destroying the painting and herself with it flickered across her mind and she was shocked by it. Why was she thinking such a thing? What was the matter with her? At the same time it gave her an insight into Horacio. What she'd felt for an instant, he sometimes felt for days at a time—weeks!

She found herself staring at her hands as if they'd betrayed her. But this had nothing to do with a bad hand or foot habit. She remembered recommending to Horacio the retraining of his hands and feet through harsh treatment. What a simplistic solution to any desperate situation. She had no understanding of the anomie that he suffered. Nor had she tried to understand, had only lectured and hectored.

When she walked back into the house, Sal was coming through the door.

"Oh God!" said Jenny. "Just what I was afraid of."

"What?"

"Your outfit. Your entire heartbreakingly bedraggled, penitential appearance."

"That's exactly it," Sal cried happily. "No one else seems to understand the look I'm trying to achieve."

"I'm not going to say one word to you until you get in the shower. I'll lay out some clean clothes for you."

"Does this mean I'm forgiven?"

"Yes."

"Good. Wait until you hear my stunning news."

"I will wait. Get in the shower."

Sal got in the shower and Jenny set out white sweatpants and a blue polo shirt for her. She put the air bag and the trashed silk outfit in a shopping bag and set it by the door. Then she decided to open a bottle of wine. Maybe if she poured enough wine in her head she could create the pristine pool.

Sal appeared, wet hair slicked back, face scrubbed and clean but blurry without the customary makeup. Jenny poured a glass for Sal and they took the wine out to the deck, Sal on the padded redwood chair, Jenny on the matching lounge. The sun was edging toward the ridge for an assignation with the fog, which was churning toward the same ridge from the sea, boiling up over the top of it, slipping down the eastern side.

"I must say, it's a relief to be clean," Sal said.

"What's your news?"

"I went to the Mill Valley Inn to try to collar Beck about your lost show and guess what?"

"What?" asked Jenny wearily.

"There was a dead man in his room."

Jenny's heart stopped and started again. She remained quiet. She drank wine.

"I didn't see it. Fran at the desk told me. They don't know who it is. Beck checked himself out a couple of hours before the maid found the body."

"How do they know it was Beck who checked out?" Jenny asked in a quavering voice.

"Well, I suppose it was the beard, the hat, the coat, the whole number. No one else looks like him around this town."

"What did the dead man look like?"

"Bald, is all I know. There was no identification on him. He wasn't necessarily murdered."

"What do you mean?"

"Well, not shot or stabbed. Could be a natural death, but who is he? What was he doing there? The receptionist said it wasn't the Mexican who's been seen frequenting Beck's room—the guy in the trailer yesterday? Beck's amigo?"

Jenny was trying to think but couldn't. "Would you please get the bottle of wine?"

No hope for the pristine pool. The roiling river of her mind was at high flood. Her brain cells were up in the treetops hoping for rescue from some passing canoe.

Horacio must not have gone away. There had been some sort of showdown between him and Harry. Who had won? Harry had been undisguised when she saw him, so maybe he was the dead man, and Horacio had donned the wig and beard to check out. Or Harry could have shaved Horacio's hair and mustache and left him there, hoping Horacio couldn't be identified. But why bother? Why not leave him as the unidentified Mexican stranger?

Jenny would have to view the body to be sure it was Harry. She would not even entertain the idea it was Horacio until she saw the body. She shuddered uncontrollably.

Sal returned and topped off their glasses. Jenny quaffed hers.

"The question is," Sal said, resettling herself, "What were you doing at the Mill Valley Inn today, going up to Beck's room, not so long before?"

"Before what? The murder? Are you suggesting I'm the murderer?"

"Well, no. It was before Beck checked out."

"Private business," Jenny replied coldly. "None of your business and don't say anything to Jeff about it."

Sal's eyes lit up. "Trouble in paradise?" she asked. "Keeping secrets from each other already? You'd better tell me what you were doing there, or I might have to ask Jeff about it."

"Are you threatening me?"

"Oh, come on Jenny. What's happened to your sense of humor? I just want to know. We used to tell each other everything."

"That was before you tried to destroy my life's work."

"You said you'd forgiven me."

"Because I felt sorry for you. Maybe I shouldn't have. I'm beginning to think you're vicious."

"Jenny," Sal wailed. "How could you speak to me that way? You always used to be so kind. It must be Jeff. He's turning you against me. You watch—he'll turn you against Mae and Gram too. He'll turn you against Abraham if he can. He wants to be the only one in your life. He wants to control you. You're already afraid of him."

Jenny winced. Was it true? She didn't want him to know she'd acted against his wishes by paying the ransom, but was it fear of his displeasure or fear of losing him because the money was gone? If that was it, then she had no trust in his affection, did she? It would be better to admit to herself she was paying him to stay with her. Better than living a lie. It was living a lie that was probably preventing her from painting. And starting my alcoholism, she added to herself refilling her glass. Okay, so Jeff was with her because of her money and there was no more money. Gram's allowance would only briefly give the appearance of money.

Did she still want him to stay if that was the case, the known case?

Yes.

Jenny guessed this meant she was already demoralized. Morally reprehensible would be next. From now on, she was going to be a morally reprehensible non-painting alcoholic.

36 SAYING HIS NAME

JEFF WAS ON A LONE RIDE, testing his new bike. It was a sweet one, his first with full suspension. He liked riding solo. Most of his recent rides had been with friends, and though he enjoyed the camaraderie and competition, it was nice to be alone with his thoughts, getting to know his new bike. It seemed to pour over the rocks, roots, and holes so that it was like riding water. He was relaxed on it—not muscling his way so much, not gritting his teeth. Instead he smiled.

He poached a single track on the bare hills that swept between the mountain and the ocean. Ahead, an oak tree spread itself above the trail and he saw a part of the tree detach itself and fall to the tall grass where it merged, was no longer rigid tree but flowing grass which, at this season was between the green and gold stage, a mauve, almost lavender. Now Jeff saw that what was merging with the grass was not a tree limb but a mountain lion. It crouched low, tail moving slightly, not looking his way. It concentrated down the hill where some deer were feeding, a family of four: buck, doe, yearling and fawn.

The mountain lion looked his way and Jeff experienced the same fear as when Beck had said "fuck you," the feeling he could die at any minute for no reason except a natural malevolence.

Hikers were warned not to follow their inclination to turn and run like hell from a mountain lion, but to remain calm and slowly back away: the bigger you looked the better. Jeff figured that on the bike he looked big.

The mountain lion may or may not have thought so, but in any case it began moving downhill toward the deer, freeing the trail for Jeff to pass, although he waited until the beast was a good distance away. Jeff waited, not because he was still scared, but because it was so wonderful to see the mountain lion, the deer, the blue swath of ocean and, in the grass, tangles of wild flowers. In spite of himself, Jeff was looking at nature.

When he got home, as he now thought of Jenny's house, he put the bike in the garage and, bounding up the steps, decided he really didn't want a romantic getaway with Jenny. He wanted to keep riding his new bike and get to work on his book idea. He'd have to buy some computer equipment. There was no reason he couldn't publish the book himself with all the technology available now to do so. He could probably set himself up for under ten thousand—peanuts for Jenny. Then he'd only have to send the books out to be bound, find a distributor, and he was in business. Then, seeing its success, a major publisher would pick up the book for some outrageous sum. Jeff wasn't just dreaming. He knew he had a winner. The book would strike a responsive chord in every small town across America.

When Jeff walked through the door, he was not met by Jenny's usual happy smiles and warm embraces. Instead he heard a snoring sound coming from the deck. He found Jenny spread-eagle on the lounge, two empty bottles of wine on the table. Her mouth was open, her tongue protruding and drool slipping from the corner of her mouth like a snail trail. She looked every one of her thirty-eight years, with another decade thrown in for good measure. Nor was her snort-like snore a pretty sound.

Jeff, fresh from his vigorous ride on the mountain and imbued with resultant virtue, was disgusted by the sight. Abraham wandered onto the deck from the bushes, sat down by the prostrate Jenny and seemed to look at her with a similar disapproval. Jeff briefly bonded with the old dog.

Well, at least she'd missed the six o'clock news and wouldn't know about the dead man in room fourteen of the Mill Valley Inn. And at least he wouldn't have to make love to her tonight.

This twice-a-day shit had to stop. It was unrealistic of her to expect it.

Jeff went back into the house, showered, and put on a pot of water for spaghetti. He'd brought his file of photographs from the newspaper. After supper he'd go over them, decide on which ones to include in his book and plan what still needed to be captured on film to tell his story of small town wrath. Hmm. Good title: *Small Town Wrath.*

When dinner was ready, he halfheartedly tried to rouse Jenny and, failing, covered her with a blanket against the cool evening. When he went to bed, he left her out there.

Jenny awoke around midnight and opened her eyes to the surprise party of the universe. It was a clear night and every planet and star had come out to play in all their varied assemblages. It was as if she'd been in her bedroom and opened her eyes to find the ceiling covered by a Michelangelo fresco—she couldn't have been more astonished and delighted. She let the radiance wash over her, cleansing her, renewing her, kindling the coals of her creative spirit, then she closed her eyes and slept until dawn, when she awoke to an apricot sky.

Jeff found Jenny making coffee. He felt guilty for having left her out on the deck when he could so easily have carried her to bed, but he brushed it aside. Instead of apologizing, he said dryly, "How are you feeling this morning?"

"Great. How about you?"

He saw that she truly did feel great and so responded in kind, telling her all about his book plans while she cooked an herb omelet. He toasted sourdough slices to go with it.

Jenny was enthusiastic about his project. Jeff's heart was moved. It was the first time he'd shared a dream with someone who responded by being one hundred percent behind him. He decided to wait on telling her about the expenses the project would incur. He'd find out the exact costs first. He wanted to leave the discussion on a creative level for now.

"What are you going to do today?" Jeff asked as they ate their breakfast.

"Well, paint, of course. After I go downtown to look at the body."

"The body?"

"Of the unidentified person at the Mill Valley Inn."

"Why?"

"To see who it is, of course." Jenny remembered Jeff's proscription of yesterday to never again mention Horacio's name, that he would leave her if she did, and added, "To be sure it isn't Horacio."

She looked at him carefully. Was he going to get up, throw down his napkin, and storm out of the house, never to return? It didn't look like he would, not by the way he was forking the next mouthful of omelet.

"Horacio," she said again, relishing the sound.

"And if it is?"

"I'm pretty certain it isn't," she said.

Jenny felt like there had been one of those power shifts he'd told her about early in their relationship. Strange. Yesterday she'd been prepared to beg, borrow, or steal to keep him with her and today—well, she didn't feel scared of losing him anymore, although she wasn't quite ready to tell him about the forsworn million. Not yet. Her new courage could be due to the fact that she was still a little drunk—not from the wine necessarily, but from the stars.

As Jeff was leaving for work he asked, "What is your portmanteau doing here by the door?"

Jenny pondered a moment, then asked, "How did you know I called it a portmanteau?"

"Huh . . . ?"

"Was it because the man in the garage called it that?"

"Well . . . "

"So now we know it was definitely Horacio"—saying his name for the third time. "No one else in the world would have called it a portmanteau but him. That's proof enough that he's alive, Jeff."

"But I didn't know it was him. How would I know that the two of you called it a fucking portmanteau, that you had little pet names for everything? Christ almighty, what did you call the refrigerator? What did you call the roof? And this damn thing"—he shoved the big wooden soldier looking cheerily down on him—"to think I carried it all the way up the stairs on our first date just so I could pass Horacio's favorite toy every time I came in and out the fucking door."

That was the fifth mention of Horacio in as many minutes, and this last one, being so loud, brought Abraham into their midst, looking inquiringly at the two of them.

"Not to mention his dog. Are we going to live with his dog the rest of our lives? This dog who only shows a sign of life at the mention of his name. The rest of the time he sleeps and farts. If the body turns out to be Horacio, I suppose you'll tell them you want his ashes in an urn for the mantle. That will complete the picture around here." Jeff slammed out the door in Jenny's face and was gone.

Jenny flinched, but then she started to laugh. Abraham looked pleased.

37 IN THE MORGUE

JENNY STARED DOWN at the body of Harry Huntington, a.k.a. Beck, a.k.a. Laveen. The crook is dead—long live the crook. He looked frightened. His mouth curved down like a tragedy mask and his brows frowned. Funny that the expression hadn't relaxed in death. The man who valued fear over love had died afraid. The shock to his system must have come from the foreign feeling of fear itself, not from whatever had scared him.

"Was it a heart attack?" she asked the police officer.

"That's what the coroner says. There's a bruise on the back of his head, but he apparently hit the mantle when he fell. Did you know him?"

"Yes." Jenny told the cop Harry's name. "His prints will be with the FBI unless they closed out his file thinking he was already dead." She didn't mention Beck.

What had Horacio felt upon seeing Harry dead again? She assumed that it was Horacio who had checked out as Beck, taking his bags, including the bag with the tainted million, so laundered by now, through the seven banks, that it was pure as a lily, pure as the new fallen snow, virgin money. He was tenderhearted enough that he'd probably felt bad for a minute, given Harry his due of a minute's mourning—more than anyone else would give him. Then he had gone who-knew-where. It didn't matter. Like Gram, Horacio was still on this earth and that was all that Jenny needed to know.

When Jenny got home there was a message from Galerie La Vigne, saying the paintings had arrived, were splendid, and that the show would be mounted in a month, as instructed by Monsieur Beck.

38 STILL SAYING HIS NAME

THREE MONTHS LATER Jenny had sold nine of the thirteen paintings to four different people and, doubting that Horacio could be all four purchasers, two at the most, she felt acknowledged. If people were willing to pay money for her work, wanted to have her paintings in their homes, she must be a good artist.

But it was Jeff who was famous. *Small Town Wrath* was selling out of the stores as fast as the distributor could get it there and, true to his prediction, a major publisher had purchased it for a lot of money. Jeff was getting rich on his own and he could leave Jenny, but he didn't. She could tell him that she had no money except Gram's allowance and what the paintings brought in, but she didn't.

They stayed together. Their lovemaking had gone from twice a day to once a day to a few times a week, which Jeff considered realistic. Fame made him more arrogant than ever; also more virile, sexy, and powerful. Jenny was still attracted to him, though she didn't love him or even like him much either. The madness of her infatuation had spent itself, had released its octopus grip, although she was still slightly entangled by its tentacles.

The giant toy soldier had been removed. Abraham languished, sleeping and farting, wandering disconsolately around the now-abandoned lot next door, the cleared area of which was already sprouting new growth.

Jeff and his publishing venture had taken over the house: phones, faxes, and office machines of every description were scattered about, and a dark room off the bedroom stank of chemicals.

He was even making noises of wanting to expand into Jenny's studio since she so rarely painted these days, but Jenny, who gave into Jeff on most fronts, dug in her heels at this, which is to say she responded, "I don't think so."

She, too, tended to wander a bit disconsolately around the next door lot and had even broken into the trailer so she could have a getaway place from Jeff, his obnoxious friends, his business and, sometimes at night, his parties, which were full of empty-headed noisy people in their twenties talking about bicycles.

She longed to get away from the continuous sound of machines, even the dishwasher that made life so much easier, especially considering the parties. The new stereo, too, was an intrusion—certainly the TV was. The house was never silent. The phone rang, and if she let the machine take messages, she had to sift through Jeff's ten before finding her one. The washing machine sloshed, the dryer whirred. Where did all the dirty clothes come from? They even had a cappuccino machine now, which sucked and burred.

The trailer was a haven, like her house used to be before Jeff.

She considered the nineteen-foot trailer hers because she'd paid a million dollars for it. Inside it, she could be herself—a morally reprehensible, non-painting alcoholic—to her heart's content, accompanied by old Abraham.

She and Jeff continued to get along well because he mostly got his way. The only time they fought was if she mentioned Horacio and she sometimes did just to prove to herself that she still had some spirit. What they fought about, as they had from day one, was whether or not Horacio was alive.

Jenny, after viewing the body, told Jeff it wasn't Horacio and Jeff told her it had to be and made her study the pictures he'd taken of the body—as if they would look different to her than had the body itself. She gave him her tremulous little speech how she would know Horacio by his little finger, which infuriated Jeff further. The one thing Jeff couldn't get Jenny to do was say that Horacio was dead, even though he knew Horacio must be. The body was Horacio's. It couldn't be anybody else's. Horacio had worked hand in glove with Beck to get the half million for the paintings and, since Beck had been seen checking out, that left Horacio to be the dead man. It was clear as day.

Jeff thought Jenny said the body hadn't been Horacio's just to annoy him, to madden him, to drive him into a temper, and then to smile at him, sometimes laugh. Jeff didn't know how she triumphed over him every time the subject came up. Sometimes he even got confused enough to get out the pictures of the dead man and wave them in her face, crying "Proof! Proof!"

Jenny could have explained it all, could have told Jeff about Harry Huntington and the rest, but didn't. Even if Jeff listened, which he wouldn't, she enjoyed this one tiny bit of power she had over him. Small satisfaction. Painting six hours a day would be more satisfying, but she was unable to paint.

Sal continued to be a thorn in Jenny's side, not because she was still talking venomously about Jeff but because she was singing his praises. Since he was famous, Sal naturally had to fawn and invite them to dinner parties. Jenny, of course, was also dinner party material, now that she'd had a Paris show.

Gram continued to be Jenny's anchor and Mae to be her darling daughter. Mae came for visits but Gram didn't. Nor had Gram invited Jenny to her house for a while. They talked on the phone, but it was difficult because Jenny was holding back her unhappiness. She had always been so open with Gram but couldn't be now because she was living a lie.

Her life narrowed to her sketchbooks, a bottle of wine, and Abraham, together in the tiny trailer under the orange madrone.

39 FALLOUT

One Saturday Mae breezed into the house and found Jenny and Jeff out on the deck having coffee and reading the morning paper, Abraham dozing at Jenny's feet.

"I can't believe I found a parking place. How come there isn't the usual crowd here today? Isn't Jeff feeling well?"

She gave Jenny a kiss, nodded to Jeff and, stooping down, nuzzled Abraham.

"Jeff hurt his foot and can't go biking for a day or two. He's grumpy," Jenny explained. "He's feeling sorry for himself. It's marvelous. So quiet."

Mae plopped herself down on Jenny's lap. "With all the people coming to the house every day, I'm surprised Jenny hasn't decided one of them is Horacio," Mae said innocently. "It's been quite a while since she thought anyone was my dad. Not since the Mexican."

"The Mexican?" Jeff looked over at the women's eyes darting from one to the other.

Jenny had never told Jeff that Horacio was the Mexican and she didn't want him to know it now that she was spending so much time in the trailer. If Jeff knew it was Horacio's trailer she had chosen as a retreat, that she had come to prefer it to her own house, it would not go over well.

At the same time she was sick to death of the mammoth lie that she was living as a phony millionaire and the litter of lies procreated by the mother lie. She knew it was living like this that kept her from painting—although some interesting things were beginning to happen in her drunken sketchbooks.

"What Mexican?"

Mae, feeling Jenny stiffen, didn't elaborate on her remark. She scrambled to her feet. " 'Scuse me. Got to make a phone call real quick. Got to pee too. And get some coffee. And then I think maybe I have an appointment downtown. Just remembered. See ya."

Jeff and Jenny glared at each other.

"The Mexican in the trailer," Jenny said. She decided to talk. "With the wound. The wound which, I suppose, was inflicted by Beck when he took the money that Horacio had taken from you. Horacio had been staying in the trailer the whole time."

Jeff clenched his jaw and managed, "Really? Tell me more."

"The lot belongs to him. It's a matter of public record. Look it up. Horacio was the man clearing the lot. He was the burglar who beat you up. My yellow kimono is hanging in the trailer's closet. And I think it was Horacio who crashed into Sal and wrapped her in the air bag."

Jenny paused as the front door slammed. Mae leaving.

Jenny drew a deep breath. "And, finally, it was Horacio who was there at the Mill Valley Inn when Beck died. Horacio made off with the million dollars. Yes, the entire million. I went ahead and paid the ransom for Horacio. So," Jenny smiled. "There it is. Horacio is alive and he has all my money."

Jenny had laid it out, simply and clearly, and felt marvelous. She didn't care what happened next. She was glad to be free of all the falsehood. She felt so free, so lightheaded, she thought she might float off the deck and into the clouds above the mountain, like a helium balloon flying upward growing ever smaller until she was only a dot, and then nothing. She was in the near-dot phase now.

Jeff calmed down. "I could see there wasn't any cash to speak of in our account. I figured you had invested the half million—and four thousand showing up monthly would be about right. But Jenny." He surprised her by coming over to her, pulling her out of the chair, and embracing her. "I don't care. I'm happy here with you, both of us getting by on what we have."

This was a surprise, but not a nice one. Jenny's festive balloon-aloft feeling deflated.

He continued, "I admit, at the outset, I just wanted a nice place to stay and I was lucky to find one with you in it. In fact," he laughed, "you're still a millionaire because that's what this house is worth, even though it's in such terrible shape. It's a million dollar fixer-upper with no mortgage. You're so naive, Jenny. I've checked it with realtors. You're on four acres here and could even subdivide.

"You want me to sell the house, or just go ahead and subdivide?"

"Neither. I only want you to realize that you could mortgage it for as much money as you want. In fact, you should. It's money going to waste otherwise, just sitting there."

Jenny was experiencing a strange, almost baffling revulsion. Her relief and happiness were turning to consternation, even fear. She had been so sure Jeff would fly into a temper and leave her forever when he learned the truth, but it turned out she was still rich and he wasn't leaving her. What was baffling was that she hadn't realized how much she wanted him to go. She wanted her house back, her life and art back. She hadn't been afraid of him leaving—she had been afraid of him staying.

She tried, "Surely you don't want to be with a woman whose money is just sitting there."

He laughed.

"Aren't you angry about Horacio being the Mexican?" she asked. "Aren't you upset that I knew and didn't say, and that I've been staying in the trailer so much?"

"I figured it was him. When I saw how you tended to his wound and I knew he must be the man I'd fought because he was so bashed up. By all rights I should have been the winner of that fight. I didn't have a mark on me and he did."

This had been an ongoing refrain of Jeff's. Now Jenny said, as she'd been wanting to every time, "Horacio is incredibly strong and fast on his feet, too. He's a wonderful fighter."

Jeff was unprovoked. "Even though he was speaking Spanish, and didn't have a stone in his mouth for disguise purposes, I recognized his voice from the garage. I know the garage guy was Horacio because instead of taking the money and sending me on my way, he lectured me about treating you decently. It was bizarre. And certainly a giveaway of his identity. However, I think I've taken his advice, don't you?"

Again Jeff tried to embrace her.

Jenny pulled away. "Then you knew he was alive when Beck asked me for the ransom money."

"Right. Boy, I have to say, I'm glad to get this all cleared up between us."

"You knew he was alive and yet you told me not to pay. You were as good as writing his death warrant."

"Jenny, you thought he was alive, hoped he was alive, imagined he was alive, but didn't know he was. So, let him be dead was my thinking."

"But didn't you feel awful when you saw the dead body, thinking it was Horacio?"

"Not really. To be honest, I was glad more than anything."

Jenny stepped away, faced him and said, almost sternly, "Jeff, I want you to leave. I don't love you. I hate living with you."

His eyes filled with anger, losing the green light that had so entranced her when she saw them first. Now they were mud-colored.

"I've never cared whether you loved me or not."

"You're a heartless person," she said. "Only looking out for yourself."

"Fuck you," he said and now, at last, after much practice, he sounded like Harry, full of menace and evil, inspiring fear. Here, all the time, in her house, and in her arms, was the Laveen she'd so hated and feared, whereas Harry himself was only a ruin of the Laveen he had been, an imitation of his previously malignant self, a personality as fragile and tenuously repaired as the skull she'd smashed.

Jeff could be so charming, full of fun, passionate, all those things Harry could never have been that she'd been bewitched. If she'd suspected Jeff's cold, calculating, heartless nature, she'd squashed the suspicion.

"I'm staying here, Jenny." Now Jeff raised his voice. "Squatter's rights. If you don't like it, sleep in your precious trailer. Or go live with Gram. Possession is nine-tenths of the law. I may not own the place, but I'm here to stay and there's nothing you can do about it. You invited me in." Now he was yelling. "You paid me to stay. If you make any complaint to anyone, I'll kill Abraham. That's the deal. Take it or leave it."

When Jenny said nothing, too shocked to speak, he tried to collect himself and just barely succeeded, saying, "If you want to go on as we have, being lovers and friends, that's fine with me. I still like you better than any woman I've ever known, and that's saying a lot. I've always been straight with you. Much more than you have with me. But now neither of us has to fake it anymore. We've laid it all on the line. Yes, I look out for myself the same as everyone else in this world, including your precious Horacio. I like what I've got and I'm keeping it."

"Okay," Jenny said. "I accept the deal." She walked out of the house leaving Jeff to wonder what deal it was she accepted, what it was he'd said in his anger that she was going along with. Probably it was the last part, about continuing on as they were, that she was accepting. Yes, that must be it.

He swore under his breath and limped into the kitchen for more coffee.

40 JEFF

A FEW DAYS WENT BY during which Jeff saw no sign of Jenny. After the first day, he figured she was sulking and would show up, but she didn't. Both Gram and Sal had called for her, so she wasn't with them. She must be in the trailer but he was damned if he was going to go look.

On the fourth day, feeling uneasy, he told himself she might be in a bad way and he should go and check out the trailer. Either that or she was waiting for him to apologize. He was willing to extend the olive branch if he had to. He wanted things back the way they were.

So he strode over there, head high and whistling, in case she was looking for him. The door was locked. He knocked on it and called, "Jenny, are you in there?"

"Yes, I'm here." Her voice was level.

"Are you all right?"

"I'm fine."

"I thought you might want to know how the book was doing." He'd discovered that no one was as interested in the book, in all its particulars, as Jenny had seemed to be. She was the only one who wanted to listen to his reviews and sales figures, the ongoing wheeling and dealing.

"I'm no longer interested. You pilloried our town by portraying our petty enmities. When I thought I loved you, I perceived the book as a call for kindliness. Now I see it as a paean to nastiness."

Jeff managed, with some difficulty, to shrug this off for now. "Well, look, the reason I'm here is to ask you to just come on home now."

"I don't want to."

"It was just a fight. It's not a big deal. There was a lot of bad stuff between us we had to get rid of. Now we can start over."

"I'll come back to the house when you've moved out." Jeff listened to this intently but couldn't detect any emotion. She could have been talking to anyone.

"We can work this out," he said.

"No we can't."

"Jenny, open the door so we can talk."

"No. I don't want to see you."

He was silent for a minute then reluctantly muttered, "I didn't mean it about killing Abraham."

"Yes you did."

"It isn't easy living with another man's dog."

"I think you've had it easy."

"So have you." He bristled.

"I accept responsibility for everything that has happened. I took you into my home, a complete stranger. I accepted Horacio's money. I lived a lie. I brought all this trouble down on my own head, and now I have to get myself out of it. Don't worry, I won't go to the police or to anyone. I won't risk Abraham's life over a stupid house."

"Are you going to live in this crummy trailer the rest of your life?"

"I love this trailer. I'm perfectly happy here for now." She sounded like she meant it. He didn't get it. It wasn't much larger than the van he'd been living in before he met her.

"Good luck, then, bitch."

Jeff stalked away, not whistling. Still, he wasn't worried. If nothing else he had a sexual hold on her. She'd give in.

But why did he want her to give in? He had the house, didn't he?

He missed her.

He missed her warm, happy nature. She was nice to live with. He missed sex with her. She was a great lover. And she was a friend. She'd been behind him on his book project, working as hard as he did, giving him good honest feedback but never, until now, putting him down.

Sure he'd wanted her house and her money, but now he wanted her, too. He wondered if he'd blown it. He should never have said anything about Abraham. She loved that dog. It was like threatening to kill her child. Bad move on his part. But he had been pissed off at the time. You can say anything in anger. Although he had meant it. Nothing would make him happier than getting rid of that mutt. Okay, so he wasn't such a nice guy. Who ever said he was? And what was so great about nice? Nice was boring. One thing he wasn't was boring. He was handsome, a hell of an athlete, smart, talented, and now he was getting rich. Did he have to be a saint besides?

He knew it wasn't only his threat to Abraham, although that was plenty. It was that he'd been willing to sell out Horacio. Why couldn't she see that anyone, if asked, would want to get rid of the competition? It wasn't as if Jeff had put a gun to the guy's head.

Still, he knew he should have played it cool about Horacio. Horacio had been out of her life and Jeff had been in solidly with nothing to worry about. Then for some reason he kept acting like a jealous idiot. Now look at the situation.

Jeff spent a week sleeping with other women to no avail. He still missed Jenny. She was the woman he wanted. He had learned a lot from her, just through propinquity. Everyone else seemed shallow.

41 SAL

SAL DROPPED BY THE HOUSE all the time, but she never found Jenny home anymore—only Jeff, if anyone. Usually the house was empty. Strange. Jenny always used to be in her studio every day from nine until one. Her schedule was carved in stone. But now she was never there. What was going on? She'd finally found success. This was no time to stop working. She should feel encouraged. Even if she hadn't sold many paintings, she'd gotten the Paris show, had been seen, gotten her name out.

One day when Sal stopped by, she caught a glimpse of Jenny walking in the next lot. "Jenny!" she called out. She saw Jenny look over with no reaction, as if she didn't recognize her.

Sal took off toward Jenny, stumbling over the rough ground in her high heels. Jenny called in a strained voice, "I'm looking for Abraham. I haven't seen him since yesterday afternoon. I'm terribly worried."

"He's probably just off prowling," said Sal, arriving at Jenny's side.

"But he hasn't been wandering much these days. He seems to want to stay by my side. We're quite inseparable."

"How does Jeff feel about that?"

Jenny didn't answer.

Sal homed in.

"Everything all right between the two of you?"

"Give it a rest, Sal."

"So there's trouble, eh? Well, I know why. You can't stand it that Jeff is having this success. You want to be the rich and famous one and have him be your adoring lover."

"Don't attribute your feelings to me, Sal."

"Admit that your show fell flat."

"I sold nine paintings. That's pretty good."

"Nine?" Sal felt a surge of the old jealousy. It was like a live thing inside her that had been happily snoozing and now was wide awake, writhing away, gnashing its teeth. "You never told me," Sal sputtered.

"Guess why."

"Jenny, I'm truly happy for your success." With the saying of it, the creature inside seemed miraculously subdued. "I'm reformed. Air Bag Therapy. I recommend it for everyone."

Jenny laughed.

"And don't forget I was looking all over for Beck to try to get your show back on track."

"That's true."

"So what do you think changed Beck's mind? I can't stop wondering."

"It's simple. Horacio probably put a gun to his head and made him call Paris."

"You mean Horacio's ghost, I assume." Sal sighed. "No man ever loved a woman the way that man loved you. And now you have Jeff crazy about you. I have to admit, I don't get it."

"Jeff doesn't love me and never did."

"Oh now, that's ridiculous."

"You were right about him from the start."

Sal wanted to have been right, of course, but at this point she didn't want Jenny to lose Jeff and become less interesting. She changed the subject. "Never mind that now. Work is more important than love. Why aren't you painting?"

"I am sketching."

"Rocks?"

"Abraham. You know how Georgia O'Keefe did her flowers up close so your eye practically goes squirming inside them? I'm doing Abraham that way so sometimes the whole picture will just be brown whorls of fur and folds, or eye and ear, or mouth and whiskers and drool. You don't know what it is at first, then you realize it's part dog, part wise, old, loyal good dog, part of the best dog who ever lived. I've even done one of his balls."

"Jenny, it sounds marvelous!"

"Thank you, Sal. Tell me how your work is going."

Sal told Jenny about her recent canvasses. They talked for a while and Jenny felt happy to be with her friend after so many weeks alone. They talked about other artists and about technique. Jenny felt enriched. Once Jenny got Sal away from gossip, she had depth and ideas.

Mae had also come to the house, seeking Jenny out, and she had been told the same dog sketches story. It was a true story, but it wasn't the whole story. But there was no use in upsetting everyone with the situation, which was something Jenny alone had to solve. Once again she was living a lie—this time to her nearest and dearest—but what could she do? Mae and Gram would be appalled to learn she'd abandoned the house to Jeff and was living in the trailer.

She couldn't see any solution to the situation except to wait it out. There was no point in changing the locks on the doors or, as Horacio had done once to a tenant who owed rent and wouldn't move out, removing the doors entirely. She didn't have the skill for that herself and she didn't want to involve anyone else. Anyhow, it might not work, since they always kept the doors unlocked anyhow.

If only she could see Gram. She couldn't talk to her on the phone but she felt she'd be able to unburden herself in person. Gram always knew what to do, had advice for any occasion, because she'd lived through them all. But every time Jenny suggested a visit, Gram put her off.

Jenny felt she could wait out Jeff indefinitely if she weren't so scared about Abraham.

42 GRAM

GRAM WORRIED ABOUT JENNY but was not in a position to help her. So she did the next best thing. She hired a detective to track down Horacio, pretty sure he'd be near Puerto Vallarta. Horacio was a man who clung to his old haunts. The detective found him easily and told him that Gram wanted to see him—that it was an emergency, and he had to come home at once.

In her Pacific Heights mansion, one of the few he hadn't burgled over the years, Horacio was ushered into her bedroom, where she sat up in bed propped against some pretty pillows. She was wearing a satin and lace bed jacket. Horacio hadn't seen one in years. Her hands were folded in front of her and she looked relaxed and calm for someone experiencing an emergency. He was struck by how large and beautiful her eyes were.

They greeted each other warmly and Gram said, "You look wonderful, Horacio. I'd forgotten what a handsome man you are."

His hair was short, returned to its own silver color. He was tanned and lean. The mustache was gone, and he flashed her his world-class smile. He'd always liked Gram.

"Thanks. You look good, too, Gram." But now he began to wonder if her eyes looked so large because she was so small. Had she always been so small? Maybe it was just that she wasn't up and about, radiating her usual subtle force. "What's up?" he asked.

"There is something terribly wrong at Jenny's house."

Horacio's good ear pricked up. His old warrior blood stirred but he stayed cool, even pretended indifference. "It's not my business. Jenny's leading her own life now."

"She has taken that unscrupulous young man into her house and now she can't get him out."

"She's always been attracted to unscrupulous men. She just turned me in for a younger model."

"Wrong. You were ostensibly dead. She was grieving. He got to her in a vulnerable moment. You have behaved intolerably, Horacio, but I won't get into all that. Jenny is in trouble but, for the first time in her life, she has not confided in me. I think she feels she has to solve this herself, but she's not very good at that. Never has been."

"You brought me all the way up here to settle a lover's quarrel?"

"It's worse than that. You know Jenny has always needed taking care of."

"Not any more. She's on her own now. She doesn't need me anymore. I heard her say so."

"Nonsense. We all will always need each other. What would life be if we couldn't depend on our friends and family to look out for us?"

"Jenny's doing great. She sold nine paintings at her Paris show."

"How many of them did you buy?"

"None. Hell, I'd already bought them once. But I did have to take over the gallery with Harry out of the picture. It wasn't easy. No one understands English over there."

"They just pretend not to." Gram smiled. "Horacio, go to Jenny's house and find out what's wrong. Jenny is never at home. I can't reach her by phone unless she calls me and I can't travel just now. As far as I can tell, from what Mae says, she's living in the little trailer you put on the adjoining lot."

"Why can't you travel?"

"Well, I'm sorry to say I'm dying."

"Damn."

"Poor Jenny will go into a complete tailspin. I haven't let on—she has enough trouble right now. That's why it was important for you to be here. To help her now and to help her in a few days or so, when I'm gone."

"This is terrible. Thank God . . . thank God you got me home."

"Yes. I was just waiting for you. Now I can let myself go at any time."

"You've got to let Jenny say good-bye, Gram."

"She'd just sit here and cry her eyes out, poor darling."

"But—"

"We'll see. Meanwhile, get going. I want a full report. Hurry!"

43 JEFF

JEFF RETURNED TO THE TRAILER, ready to beg, ready to say what he'd never said to anyone.

"Jenny?"

"Yes?"

"Please come home. I want us to be together." He drew a deep breath and managed to blurt out, "I love you."

"I hate you," answered the steady voice from within.

"I can't believe this. I just said I love you. And I mean it. It has nothing to do with the house or the money or anything but you yourself."

"Then prove you love me by moving out and never showing your face around here again."

Jeff had a hopeful thought. "Jenny, I don't think you're feeling like yourself right now. Didn't you used to have breakdowns? Maybe this has put you over the edge. Come out of the trailer and into my arms. Let me make you well. Let me make love to you, Jenny. Everything can be like it was."

"Please leave me alone. I've kept my part of the deal. It wasn't written in your part that you would get to beleaguer me here in my small retreat. Go away and don't come back."

"I haven't left the house, Jenny, because I'm waiting there for you."

"Don't make it sound like you're some noble suffering lover when you are nothing more than a cold, calculating, greedy man who has threatened me out of my own home. I'm willing to bide my time here until you go because I am so glad to be away from you and because I accept that this situation is all my fault in some ways. Even if it isn't, I don't care."

That was what Jeff couldn't get a handle on, that she didn't care. She was just going along, living each day and apparently not suffering in the least. It was Jeff who was upset and lonely and angry. He had seen her out and about the trailer, sketching, working in the little garden she'd planted, or hanging out clothes on the line she'd strung on the tree branches. He'd watched her walking with Abraham over the hill and back again, seen her drive off in the Alfa and return.

Most of the time he was home he spent watching her through binoculars. When he came home from a bike ride or business, he looked for signs of her having been in the house, but there never were any. She didn't love him, didn't miss him, didn't care.

But he cared. And he decided to make her care, too. He was hurt, angry, wronged, not to mention foiled. It seemed to him that if he got rid of Abraham she would see how upset he was. And, finally, she would feel upset too.

44 HORACIO

HORACIO WAS UP IN THE MADRONE. When Jeff asked Jenny to come home, said he wanted to be with her, said "I love you," Horacio was impressed. He himself had not uttered such winning words at the breakup between the two of them. He'd been able to muster "Don't go," to Jenny but that was the best he could do: a pitiful "don't go."

So he was shocked when Jenny cruelly replied, "I hate you." Horacio rustled the tree leaves indignantly. Here was a guy opening his heart to her, not an easy thing to do, and she'd brutally slapped him down.

Then Jeff retorted brilliantly with the suggestion that she might be having a nervous breakdown. Now why hadn't Horacio thought of that when she was leaving him? Of course she was sensitive on the nervous breakdown issue, and in truth she'd been mentally healthy for years but it wouldn't hurt to suggest that a woman must be certifiable to want to leave a guy such as he. Then, without missing a beat, Jenny shot back with the line about Jeff being a cold, calculating, greedy person. These were serious crimes she'd indicted Jeff of, making Horacio's own crime of taintedness look a mere misdemeanor. The poor stiff probably hadn't done anything more greedy than say he wanted his own yacht for Jenny to get all sniffy with him and start nagging at him how he should be more concerned with giving to the poor. She had probably decreed that she wasn't going to have anything more to do with him—that, as far as she was concerned, their orgy was over, and had stomped off to the trailer. As for the cold and calculating angle, Horacio needed more information but Jeff didn't sound all that cold when he asked her to come into his arms so he could make love to her on the spot.

But Gram had said Jeff threatened Jenny out of the house, and here she was, living in the trailer. Horacio wondered what sort of threat Jeff had made? Get out of this house or I'll . . . what? Kill you? It didn't sound like that, since he was begging her to come back.

All in all, Horacio had to say, he felt like Jenny was in charge and didn't need his help a damned bit. Much as he'd like to charge in and save her, Horacio couldn't see that Jenny needed him, and he didn't want to make her feel like she did, since she was doing so well holding off her supposed tormenter by herself. This was a ticklish business. Gram obviously wanted him and Jenny back together before she died, and God knows he wanted it too. But it didn't look to him as though Jenny was finished with Jeff and he didn't want to go barging in, making an ass of himself. Timing was everything.

It was a while before he got out of the tree and back to the city, and then it turned out Gram was having a bad spell and couldn't see him for a while. Friends and family were flocking around but not being admitted.

When he was ushered into the bedroom, she was hooked up to an IV with, she said, her own morphine supply. "I decided I'd toughed it out long enough. Now I feel great," she said. "What's the news?"

Horacio reported what he had heard. Gram was disgusted. "You were so busy nursing your own grievances about Jenny that you didn't apply your celebrated intuition to her problem. What I'm hearing, ignoring faulty interpretations, is this: Jenny has retreated to the trailer because Jeff has done something unforgivable. Jeff feels cheated of her presence. He wants her back. He has humbled himself and she has virtually kicked him in the teeth so now he is really going to get back at her. He is a man who will not be thwarted, who gets what he wants when he wants it, or else. He is a dangerous person, Horacio. Jenny has loaded the weapon and pointed it at herself."

"But you should have heard her, Gram. Jenny was hanging tough. She's a stand-up woman now."

"I haven't the strength to argue. You must go back right now, observe carefully, and act if necessary. I only hope you're not too late."

Horacio left her room shaking his head, thinking, *women!*

Meanwhile, Jenny still couldn't find Abraham and was frightened. What if Jeff, in his frustration, had carried out his threat? The only thing that gave her hope was that there was no body. If he'd done it, the whole point would be for her to find out, so he would be determined to leave the body where she'd see it.

It was possible Abraham had been in an accident or even gone off to die by himself. He certainly hadn't been well, hugging her side as he had been, so out of character for an independent, wanton rover.

When he hadn't shown up by nighttime, it occurred to her he could be at the house, shut in accidentally. She didn't want to go there. It would be awful if Jeff saw her coming, and thought she was returning to him. She had vowed she would never set a foot in the house until he was gone.

But there was nowhere else to look. And what if Abraham were a prisoner there? He didn't bark. She'd never know. And even if he could howl, he wouldn't, being such a stoic dog. When it grew dark, she dressed in dark jeans and jersey and skulked over to the house to see what she could see.

When Horacio arrived at the trailer a few minutes later, it was lit but empty, and he figured she must have gone to the house. He followed her over, heading for his old stomping ground, the roof, for some serious skylight peeping.

45 REUNITED

IT WAS A MOONLESS NIGHT. Stars huddled between clouds. Jenny, groping her way, checked the garage first. Abraham wasn't there. The van and the three bicycles were there, which meant Jeff was home. She ran up the steps, walked quietly into the house searching the different rooms for Abraham. She put her head around the bedroom door and quickly ducked back. The light was on. Jeff was reading in bed.

She backed away.

There was no sign of Abraham anywhere. She walked to the studio. It was empty of life, her abandoned Constellation still enshrouded in the white cloth. Then she thought to look in the little lavatory, but the door wouldn't open beyond a few inches. Abraham's body was blocking it. He had been wedged into the small bathroom and was lying on the floor. She couldn't get to him. She hated to hurt him, but she shoved until there was room enough to slip through.

Jenny crouched over Abraham. His eyes were closed but hearing her voice, he opened them, looked up at her, moaning softly. Jenny examined him, but he appeared unharmed except that he must be hungry and dehydrated from being in this stifling little place, possibly for twenty-four hours. Jeff had closed the toilet so Abraham couldn't drink. This would have been a cruel murder, and one that would look like plain old age, one that couldn't be proved. And Jeff was carelessly reading in bed while the old dog starved.

Jenny felt a rush of anger and hatred that blinded and deafened her. Everything turned a watery black with red around the edges and her ears roared as if her brain fluid was forming a maelstrom. She waited for the anger to pass. She let it flow through her, out and away, while leaning against the doorjamb, breathing deeply. When her senses returned she got an idea. She saw her way out. She knew what to do. It was the only thing and it was the perfect solution.

"I'm sorry I didn't find you sooner," she said to Abraham. "Can you walk? We've got to get you out of here. Oh, Abraham, forgive me for ever letting this terrible man into our life." Abraham couldn't stand up. She pulled him out of the lavatory and got a bowl from the studio to put water in. She raised his head so he could drink. Most of it spilled but she got some down his throat, reviving him a little. He tried to rise onto his paws but couldn't. Jenny half-carried, half-dragged him out through the studio door that opened onto the yard, taking him as far as she could. She went back and got the water bowl, and left it by Abraham's head. "Try to drink. I have to leave for a little while, but I'll be back."

Horacio, on the roof, had also seen Jeff in bed alone, reading. Scampering lightly from skylight to skylight, he tried to pinpoint where Jenny might be. He couldn't see her in any of the rooms, including the studio, the roof of which he now stood on. Then he heard a noise beyond the studio, outside. He ducked and crawled to the roof's edge. Looking down he barely made out a figure dragging something through the grass, finally disappearing into the dark. Good Lord. Had she killed Jeff?

Crawling so as not to silhouette himself against the sky, he made his way across the roof to the opposite side, above Jenny's bedroom, where he'd last seen Jeff. His knees gave out half way and when he tried to do a squat-walk it was worse. He was definitely going to give up thieving for Jenny's sake.

Jeff was still there in the bedroom, alive and reading. This was puzzling. What had Jenny been dragging?

Jenny, meanwhile, returned to the living room, walking softly. She climbed up on a chair and took the portrait of her father down from the wall, carrying it outside through the studio and bringing it to Abraham, who was lying motionless in the grass just as she had left him.

Dispersing clouds revealed a sliver of crescent moon, which lit the thickety glen with blue and silver. Again she tried to help Abraham drink but although she got the liquid in his mouth he couldn't seem to swallow. And now he didn't open his eyes when she spoke. She lay her head on his breast, heard the slow thump of his good old heart and, after a little while of wetting his fur with her tears, she heard it rumble to a stop.

Horacio retraced his crawling pattern across the roof and on the way caught sight of Jenny taking down her father's portrait. He noticed that her previously charming living room was full of office machines. She seemed to be heading again for the studio and he tried to keep pace with her from above. This was getting exhausting. He stood up, not caring if he was seen, stretched out the kinks, and walked normally.

He saw Jenny emerge from the studio lugging the picture, taking off in the same general direction as before. The combination of incidents was baffling.

Presently, Jenny reappeared at the door. In the studio, she hefted a huge can of turpentine then walked through the house, slopping it around. Good God! So this was how she was going to kill the greedy, cold, calculating lover—burn the house down around his ears!

It was time for Horacio to step in. And as Commander Gram had ordered, to act.

He descended from the roof by his faithful tree, swinging down branch by branch then dropping lightly to the ground. Once again he felt graceful, strong, and young. Maybe there were some thefts left in the old boy yet—or heists, as Jenny would say. He loved climbing up and down trees in the dark, behaving like grown men hadn't for a million or so years.

Once on the ground, he ran to the front door, pushing it open. The house reeked of turpentine. Didn't Jeff have any sense of smell?

The love of his life was busy with her task. "Jenny!" he whispered.

She looked up, eyes wide and startled. "Horacio!" A joyful grin spread over her face. She put down the can and ran into his arms. They held each other tightly in a slow larky dance. There were some kisses too. Time stood still. Finally Horacio spoke, whispering in her ear.

"Jenny, I want to help you."

"That's okay," she whispered back. "I'm almost done."

"But I want to help you not do it. I want to stop you."

"You can't stand in my way, Horacio. This is my business."

It was hard to talk so intensely in whispers. They both kept almost voicing. Horacio tried to talk slowly and calmly, which was difficult with all the turpentine fumes and feeling at any moment the house might explode.

"Harry is dead. Really dead this time. I checked."

"I know. I checked too. I went to the morgue. He's definitely dead."

"Aren't you glad to know that you hadn't killed him in the first place, and that you no longer have to fear him because he's really gone?"

"Yes, I'm glad, but what does that have to do with this?"

"You suffered so long, thinking you'd killed someone even though he was evil."

"I did. You have no idea. I could never forgive myself for taking a human life. But Horacio, can we talk about this later? I'm busy right now."

"So why kill Jeff, who isn't half as evil? It isn't worth it. No matter how badly he treated you. Don't do it, Jenny."

Jenny's whisper was shocked. "I'm not going to kill him, Horacio. I'm just going to burn the house down."

"But he's in the house. He's in the bedroom reading. He's flammable."

"I know that," she whispered annoyed. "Of course I'm going to warn him just before I torch it. I have it all planned down to the last second. But I don't want to give him time to save any of his machines. I want him to run for his life, empty-handed, and never return. It's the perfect way to get him out of here."

"But you'll lose your house."

"Believe me, it's worth it."

"Jenny—this is a bad hand and foot habit. Time to chastise your hands and make them obedient to your reason. In fact, give me your hands and I'll slap the hell out of them."

Jenny giggled. "This isn't a habit. I never burned a house down before."

"Well don't start now. And what was it you dragged from the studio?"

Jenny wasn't ready to tell Horacio the bad news, knowing it would tear him apart.

"What's going on here?" Jeff appeared before them, wrapped in his terry cloth robe. "Jenny, is that you? But who's this with you? And what's with that stench?"

"I'm Horacio."

"So Jenny was right. All this time I thought she was just trying to infuriate me. Ha!" He laughed. "The great Horacio, in person. The two immortal lovers, reunited at last. Ha!"

"I'm burning down the house, Jeff," Jenny said, loud and clear. "Get out while you can."

"Is that so?" he replied coolly. "It seems a little extreme but—well, I'm out of here. Just give me a sec to get dressed." Jeff turned for the bedroom.

"That wasn't any good at all," said Jenny, almost in tears. "I had this great plan to walk into the bedroom, splash the stuff all around the bed, make a torch out of newspaper and tell him he had twenty seconds. You wrecked it, Horacio. What are you doing here anyhow?"

"Why not give up the idea, since it's all wrecked?"

"Maybe I should. Although I don't even want to live here anymore. It's totally—"

"Tainted?"

"I never want to hear that word again."

There was a loud report, then an ear-shattering explosion from the bedroom. Flames leapt through the door, towering toward them, blasting heat, with toxic acrid smoke furling around the bloody orange.

"He's fired the chemicals from his darkroom," Jenny screamed.

"Quick, the door!" Horacio turned her around and pushed her. "This place is a bomb. The studio door, not the front. It's closer."

They ran to the studio, the flames at their heels, the house exploding around them. The door was open and they blasted through, airborne, landing on top of each other on the dishevelled tangle of long wild grass. Horacio scrambled to his feet, took Jenny in his arms and kept running as the house continued to burst into fiery fragments behind them, the fire like a live thing stamping about dementedly throwing burning house parts into the air as if to express rage at their escape. Horacio set her down when they were safely away from the conflagration, hoping the fire engines would come before the entire hill caught fire. "I'm going after the son of a bitch. He's probably down in the garage, loading his bicycles into the van. I'm going to kill him."

He started away but Jenny tackled his legs, pulling him down. He fell flat on his face uttering a stream of obscenities. Struggle as he might, he couldn't free himself from her ferocious grasp. "No, Horacio, it's not worth it. I won't let you. I'm stopping you like you stopped me, even though you were misinformed."

"This is different. He tried to kill us." Horacio tried to pry her fingers from his ankles but she was like an octopus.

"It isn't different. Not at all. It's the same. Please. We have each other. He doesn't matter any more. He's gone. Let's forget him. All I wanted was for him to be gone. Now he is."

Horacio subsided. She was right.

They lay in each other's arms as the sirens' wails grew loud.

"The firemen would have found our bodies and the turpentine can and think we'd been caught by our own arson," Horacio grumbled. "Jeff knew that. He'd be in the clear."

"Maybe he wasn't even thinking. He was just so mad that I'd vanquished him and that you were with me. Maybe he thought I was going to burn him out without warning him. Please let's forget it. I hope the trailer is okay. All my sketches."

Horacio sat up abruptly. "Abraham! What about Abraham? He wasn't in the house,was he?" Suddenly Horacio remembered the heavy load Jenny had dragged away, which began to assume doglike proportions in his mind. Tears filled his eyes. His throat constricted. He choked and coughed.

"Abraham is fine," Jenny said shakily. "We'll talk about Abraham later. There's so much to tell, sweetheart. It's been such a long time and, when you were the Mexican, I never got to talk to you, really. You were always talking Spanish or talking with a stone in your mouth."

"I'm still the Mexican. It's just my hair turned gray."

"I feel so tired now. We'll talk later, okay? Let's go home to the trailer."

"Yes." Horacio helped her to her feet. They would talk later. She would tell him about Abraham and then he would tell her about Gram. And then, well, they'd just have to look out for each other, like they always had.

Like they were doing now.

THE END

ABOUT THE AUTHOR

Susan Trott lives with her husband in a Mill Valley cottage and a Sausalito fishing boat. This is her tenth novel.